从经典作家进入历史

希尼在都柏林家中，一九八三年（Thierry Martinot 摄）

希尼出生于北爱尔兰德里郡。他的第一本诗集《一个博物学家之死》初版于一九六六年，后又出版了诗歌、批评和翻译作品，使他成为他那一代诗人中的翘楚。一九九五年，他获得诺贝尔文学奖；两度荣获惠特布莱德年度图书奖（《酒精水准仪》，1996；《贝奥武甫》，1999）。由丹尼斯·奥德里斯科尔主持的访谈录《踏脚石》出版于二〇〇八年；他的最后一本诗集《人之链》获得二〇一〇年度前瞻诗歌奖最佳诗集奖。二〇一三年，希尼去世。他翻译的维吉尔《埃涅阿斯纪》第六卷在其去世后出版（2016），赢得批评界盛誉。

◇中英双语版◇

田野工作

迷失的斯威尼

[爱尔兰] 谢默斯·希尼 著　朱玉 译

广西师范大学出版社
·桂林·

Field Work by SEAMUS HEANEY

First published in 1979. First published in this edition in 2001.

Sweeney Astray by SEAMUS HEANEY

First published in 1983. This edition, with revisions, first published in 2001.

This edition arranged with Faber and Faber Ltd. through Big Apple Agency, Inc., Labuan, Malaysia

Simplified Chinese edition copyright © 2024 Guangxi Normal University Press Group Co., Ltd.

All rights reserved.

著作权合同登记号桂图登字：20 - 2024 - 003 号

图书在版编目（CIP）数据

田野工作；迷失的斯威尼：汉、英／（爱尔兰）谢默斯·希尼著；朱玉译. —桂林：广西师范大学出版社，2024.5

（文学纪念碑）

书名原文：Field Work／Sweeney Astray

ISBN 978 - 7 - 5598 - 6929 - 6

Ⅰ．①田… Ⅱ．①谢… ②朱… Ⅲ．①诗集-爱尔兰-现代-汉、英 Ⅳ．①I562.25

中国国家版本馆 CIP 数据核字（2024）第 090513 号

田野工作·迷失的斯威尼：汉、英

TIANYE GONGZUO · MISHI DE SIWEINI: HAN、YING

出品人：刘广汉　　策 划：魏 东　　责任编辑：魏 东 程卫平

助理编辑：钟雨晴　　装帧设计：赵 瑾

广西师范大学出版社出版发行

（广西桂林市五里店路9号　　邮政编码：541004）
（网址：http://www.bbtpress.com　　　　　　　　　　　　）

出版人：黄轩庄

全国新华书店经销

销售热线：021 - 65200318　021 - 31260822 - 898

山东临沂新华印刷物流集团有限责任公司印刷

（临沂高新技术产业开发区新华路1号　邮政编码：276017）

开本：889 mm × 1 194 mm　1/32

印张：10.875　　　　字数：326 千

2024 年 5 月第 1 版　　2024 年 5 月第 1 次印刷

定价：76.00 元

田野工作

1979

给卡尔和简·米勒

目录

致　谢

　　感谢以下报刊的编辑，本书中的一些诗歌曾首发于这些报刊：

　　《安泰》、《密码》、《文汇》、《诚实的阿尔斯特人》、《爱尔兰评论》、《爱尔兰时报》、《倾听者》、《小小词语机》、《火星》、《新评论》、《纽约客》、《纽约书评》、《巴黎书评》、《诗歌时间》(BBC广播)、《威尔士诗歌》、《展望》、《塞沃尼评论》、《泰晤士诗歌》、《门槛》和《泰晤士报文学增刊》。

　　《贝格湖滨》中的但丁《炼狱篇》引文选自企鹅版译本，译者为多萝西·L.塞耶斯(1955)。

　　《挽歌》与《残余》曾刊于鹿野出版社的一本限量版诗集。《格兰摩尔十四行诗》曾由查尔斯·塞鲁兹奇出版在《树篱学校》(雅努斯出版社)里。

牡　蛎

我们的贝壳在盘子里咔嗒。
我的舌头是盈满的三角洲，
我的软腭缀满星光：
当我品味咸咸的昴星团
猎户俄里翁把脚伸进水中。

活生生被侵犯
它们躺在冰床上：
双壳动物：裂开的球体
以及海洋调情的叹息。
数百万牡蛎被撕扯、剥裂并散落。

我们驱车前往那海岸
穿过花朵与石灰岩
在那里，我们为友谊举杯，
在茅屋和瓷器的清凉中
贮酿完美的记忆。

越过阿尔卑斯，埋进干草和积雪，
罗马人拖着他们的牡蛎南下罗马：

我看到潮湿的驮篮吐出
叶状边唇、被盐水蜇痛的
大量特供品

并懊恼于我的信任不能安栖
于澄朗的光，像诗歌与自由
从大海中倾身。我故意吃下
这一天，好让它浓烈的味道
催发我成为动词，纯粹的动词。

三联画

1. 杀戮之后

他们在那儿，仿佛我们的记忆将其孵化，
仿佛那些不安的缔造者复活：
两个持步枪的年轻人在山上，
亵渎且振奋如同他们的器械。

谁为我们的动荡抱歉？
谁曾梦想我们可能共居
风雨、擦亮的光和风干的石头？
玄武岩，血，水，墓碑，蚂蟥。

在那中性原初的孤独中
从布兰顿到敦塞弗里克
我想起小眼睛的幸存花朵，
那被渴慕的、未受侵扰的幽兰。

我看见码头边的石屋。
充足的空间。宽阔的窗光。
心振奋。你走了二十码

到那些船边买鲭鱼。

而今天一个女孩走进我们家
提着满满一篮新鲜的土豆，
三个紧实的绿甘蓝，还有胡萝卜，
上面的缨叶和泥土依然清新。

2. 西比尔[①]

我的舌移动，一个摇摆松懈的合叶。
我对她说，"我们未来会怎样？"
如同被遗忘的井水可能
在清晨的爆炸后震荡

或一道裂缝攀上山墙，
她开始说话。
"我想我们目前的样态注定要改变。
狗被困。蜥蜴退化。蚍蜉。

除非宽恕找到勇气和语声，
除非戴头盔的流血的树木
变绿并张开婴拳般的幼芽
而污染的岩浆孕育出

明亮的仙女……我的人民想着钱
并谈论天气。石油钻塔哄骗他们把未来
寄托于唯利是图的钻杆。沉默
成群涌入渔船的回声探测器。

[①] 古希腊神话中的女先知。(本书脚注皆为译者注)

我们长久以来侧耳倾听的大地

被剥了皮或起了茧，它的内脏

被蒙上一种不敬的征兆。

我们的岛屿充满令人不安的噪音。"

3. 在水边

在德弗尼什我听到沙锥鸟鸣
以及守门人在钟楼下念诵
哀歌。雕刻的僧侣头像
碎裂如面包屑落在水上。

在博阿岛，眼目神圣、嘴巴性感的石像
嵌在坟冢间，两面，洞开，
以沉默回答我的沉默。
盛雨水的圣水钵。诅咒。

从马岛的一块冰冷炉石
我张望敞开的烟囱外的天空
聆听一架军用直升机
巡航时的密集转动。

一柄锤子和一个布满蛛网的破水罐
躺在窗台上。我全部的身心
想要躬身，要献祭，
要赤脚，像胎儿且悔过，

并在水边祈祷。

我们怎样先爬行再行走！我想起
直升机的阴影笼罩我们纽里的游行
惊恐的、不可逆转的脚步。

图姆路

一天清晨我遇见一支装甲车队，
在强悍的轮胎上一路啼鸣，
全都用折断的赤杨枝条伪装，
戴耳机的士兵驻守塔上。
他们要沿着我的路走多久，
仿佛他们拥有这些路？整个村子都沉睡。
我有通行权，田野，我照管的牛群，
敞棚里装有干草耙的拖拉机，
粮窖，冷闸，湿石瓦，茅屋顶的
绿与红。我该跑去告诉谁，
他们所有的后门都虚掩
为等候带来噩耗的人，凌晨时分的来客，
在预料之中，或许也被拒之门外？
播撒种子的人，立墓碑的人……
哦，战车的驭手，俯在沉睡的机枪之上，
它依然在此，你经过时就发出震荡，
那隐形的、不倒的大地中心。

一杯水

她曾经每天早晨来汲水
像老蝙蝠在田野上蹒跚而过：
水泵的百日咳，水桶声清脆
以及水满时的缓缓渐弱，
宣告她的出场。我想起
她的灰围裙，像满满水桶
那斑斑白瓷；我想起
她高音的吱呀如水泵的手柄。
夜晚的满月攀上她的山墙
又返回她的窗内并躺在
她放在桌面的水上。
我再度轻轻啜饮，为了
忠于她杯上的训诫，
"勿忘施者"，正从杯沿褪却。

贝格湖滨

悼念科拉姆·麦卡特尼[①]

> 在这小岛四周，在底下
>
> 遥远的海滨，那里碎浪扑拍，
>
> 高高的灯芯草生于泥沙。
>
> 但丁，《炼狱篇》，第一歌，第100—103行

离开加油站闪烁的白光

和田野间几盏孤独的街灯

你驶上通往纽敦哈密尔顿的群山，

穿过菲尤斯森林，曝露星辰之下——

沿着那条路，一条高而荒芜的朝圣者小径，

斯威尼曾在此逃离地涌的群魔，

流血的头颅、山羊胡和狗眼睛

在他面前齐现，撕咬并尖叫。

是什么在你前方闪烁？一个伪路障？

红灯摇晃，突然的刹车和熄火的

发动机，说话声，蒙面的头和冷酷的枪？

或在你的后视镜中，尾随的车前灯

---

① 科拉姆·麦卡特尼（Colum McCartney），希尼的远房表兄，一九七五年被联合派准军事团体谋杀。希尼本人并不认识他。

突然逼近并示意你停下，

那里你不为人知也远离你所知的：

贝格湖的低地黏土和水域，

教堂岛的尖塔，紫杉柔和的林线。

那里你常听到屋后传来枪声，

早在起床时间之前，是狩猎野鸭者

出没于金盏花和芦苇之间，

当你穿过湖滨赶牛回家，

那些空弹壳依然使你害怕：

刺鼻，铜色，生殖器，射过的。

因为你和你家以及你家和我家都在回避，

说一种古老的合谋者的言语

而不能抽响鞭子或及时行乐：

大嗓门的庖丁，牧人，触摸

干草堆和牲畜腿的人，牛棚里的交谈者，

墓园迟缓的仲裁者。

穿过你那片湖滨，牛儿正趴在

清晨的雾霭中吃草

而现在它们将不惑的凝视

转向我们的艰难跋涉，莎草作响，

浑身露水。像一面刀刃磨得

锃亮的钝刀，贝格湖在薄雾下隐隐闪光。

我转身，因为你刷刷的脚步

在我背后停下，只见你跪倒在地
头上和眼里都是血和路边的垃圾，
于是跪在你面前盈盈的草中
收集一捧捧冰冷的露水
清洗你，兄弟。我用苔藓擦拭你，
纤柔如低云散落的细雨。
我从你的臂下抬起你并将你平放。
用重发绿芽的灯芯草，我编织
绿色的圣袍罩住你的寿衣。

来自北安特里姆的明信片

纪念肖恩·阿姆斯特朗[①]

一个孤影从一道

纤细的索桥上挥手

桥的绳索和板条

危险地悬挂在

山顶和柱岩之间。

十九世纪的风。

红藻采集者。海滨剪秋罗。[②]

给你的明信片，肖恩，

那是你，孤身摇晃，

顽皮，也有些恐惧，

蓄雇佣兵的胡子

拖着哔叽燕尾：

卡里克索桥

棕黄照片上的代笔。

或应是你的船屋

---

① 希尼在贝尔法斯特女王大学时的朋友，于北爱动乱之初被
杀害。

② "Sea campions"，按俗名直译为"海滨剪秋罗"。学名是
"silene uniflora"，中文通用译名为"海滨蝇子草"。

装修民族风，

充满大麻味？

我们会发现你吗

在民主而温暖的板条码头旁

在索萨里托的

暮色与吉他间？

叛道者复出，

无人地带的王子

头在云霄或沙里，

你是镇上的

小丑社工

直到你坦率的前额拦截

一颗下午茶时间的近距子弹。

从你地上的鲜血起来。

这儿有另一条船

在湖畔的草丛，

炭烟，铁丝围起的养鸡场——

你期望但未找到的地方社群。

现在给我背《威廉·布洛特》[1]，

唱《卡拉巴》[2]

或者唱亨利·乔伊·麦克拉肯[3]

他在谷物市场的绞刑架上

亲吻他的玛丽·安。

或唱巴利城堡市集。

"给我们来首清唱！"

"如果你忘了调子

那就扯脖子嚷。"

然而你嗓音中有些什么

几乎封闭了。

你的声音是被困扰的布道坛

引领被它

---

①《威廉·布洛特》(*William Bloat*)，一首滑稽讽刺的歌谣，作
者是雷蒙德·卡尔佛特（Raymond Calvert，1906-1959），作于
一九二六年，讲述了新教徒威廉·布洛特如何杀死天主教妻子
的故事。这首歌谣的创作受到贝尔法斯特天主教与新教之间冲
突的影响。

②《卡拉巴》(*Calabar*)，爱尔兰民歌，讲述"卡拉巴号"船遭遇
海难的不幸事件。希尼的好友戴维·哈蒙德就经常唱这首歌。

③亨利·乔伊·麦克拉肯（Henry Joy McCracken，1767-1798），
一七九八年起义中的领导人物，为建立独立民主的爱尔兰共和
国，领导天主教徒和长老派成员在安特里姆反抗英国政府。失
败后被送上军事法庭，并在贝尔法斯特谷物市场执行绞刑。

围困的旋律，

独立，匆匆，不超验的

阿尔斯特——古老的礼仪

和古老的布什米尔斯威士忌，

苏打燕麦饼，浓茶，

新绳，岩盐，羽衣甘蓝，

土豆面包和忍冬牌香烟。

吹过边防关卡

水泥孔的风。

冷钢板钉成的和平线。

十五年前，就在这十月，

簇拥在你的地板上，

第一次，我把手臂绕过

玛丽的肩。

"哦，贾斯珀先生，别碰我！"[1]

你从对面吼我，

领唱，挥洒中把酒斟满。

---

[1] 当时的流行歌曲（"Oh Sir Jasper Do Not Touch Me!"）。

伤亡者

一

他总是独自喝酒

朝着高高的货架

竖起沧桑的拇指，

再来一杯朗姆

黑加仑，不必

提高他的嗓音；

或抬一抬眼睛

以不引人注意的哑剧

比划开瓶盖的动作

即可点一瓶烈性黑啤；

打烊时他会

穿着防水靴、戴着鸭舌帽

走入阵雨的黑夜，

领救济金的养家者

但生来闲不住。

我爱他全部的风度，

稳健而狡黠，

不动声色的机智，

渔夫敏锐的眼睛

和善于观察的后背。

他无法理解

我的另类生活。

有时，坐在高凳上，

忙着用刀切

一块口嚼烟草

而顾不上看我，

在痛饮后的间歇

他提起诗歌。

有时只有我俩

我总是很小心

避免优越感，

设法用伎俩

把话题转向鳗鱼

或马匹马车的学问

或者临时派爱尔兰共和军。

但我这试探的技艺

他转过去的后背也察觉：

在德里十三人

被枪杀的三夜后

人人都遵守宵禁

他却外出喝酒

于是被炸成碎片。

墙上写着："**伞兵团：十三**

博格赛德：零。"那个星期三

人人都屏住

呼吸并颤抖。

二

那是个寒冷

死寂的日子，风吹起

白法衣和黑法衣：

淋着雨，覆着花

灵柩接着灵柩

从拥挤的大教堂门口

仿佛漂浮而出

如缓流上的花朵。

共同的葬礼

展开它的襁褓，

包裹、扎紧

直到我们被牢牢绑起

如围成一圈的兄弟。

但他不会被自己人

强行留在家中

不管接到什么恐吓电话，

不管什么黑旗飘动。

我看见他转身

在被轰炸的犯罪地点

他尚可辨识的脸

露出懊悔与恐惧，

他陷入绝境的无畏凝视

在火光中炫目。

他走了好几里，

因为他嗜饮如鱼，

每晚，本能地

游向温暖亮灯

之地的诱饵，

模糊的网与低语

在烟雾缭绕的

杯盏间游移。

他犯了什么错

当他昨夜打破

我们部族的同谋？

"既然你应该是

受过教育的人，"

我听见他说，"帮我

解出那道题的正确答案。"

三

我错过了他的葬礼，

那些安静的步行者

以及一旁的私语者

从他的巷子鱼贯而出

涌向灵车

体面的轰鸣……

他们与引擎同步

它一向拖沓

惯于表达

平缓的安慰，

鱼线举起，摩拳

擦掌，冷阳光

映在水上，陆地

聚在雾下：那天清晨

我被拉上他的船，

螺旋桨旋转，转

慵懒的深水为白浪，

我和他品尝自由。

早早出发，稳稳地

从水底拉网，

批判渔获，也微笑

当你找到合适的节奏

将你，一里一里缓缓地，

引入你专属的领地

在某处，很远，彼岸……

嗅黎明的归来者，

子夜的涉雨者，

再问我一次。

獾

当那只獾闪过
进入另一个花园
你伫立，在威士忌的微醺中，
觉得自己刚刚惊扰了
某种轻柔的回归。

被谋杀的死者，
你想。
但难道不会是
某个被暴力撕碎的少年
在摇篮与爆炸之间
嗅探失落的什么，
在那些窗子敞开的夜晚，
堆肥在后院冒烟？

显灵被视为征兆。
在另一座房子我倾听
月桂下沉闷的击声
听见低语的启示
关于朦胧的爱敬。

甚至通过尸体读出

那些獾已来过。

臭名昭著的一只

躺在路边毫发无伤。

昨晚的一只迫使我刹车

但出于恐惧而非敬意。

带着獾穴的凉意

和它夜奔的气息，

蕨类王国的精灵

在我隐蔽的心里

现出原形：

猪科

和通常描绘的样子不同。

选择不爱呈现在

我们眼前的生命有多危险？

它结实肮脏的身体

和擅自闯入的爬行。

它骨子里的智慧。

这无可置疑的童仆的肩膀

也可能是我自己的。

歌手的家

当他们说卡里克弗格斯，我听见
采盐者的尖镐凝霜的回声。
我想象它，在地洞发出寒光，
一个光筑的镇区。

我们还能说些什么
用魔法召唤大地上的盐？
太多来了又去
本该晶莹且被保存

还有宜人的天气
形成事物的纹理，
季节和贮藏的气息，
是我们将得的全部。

于是我对自己说圭巴拉
它的音乐撞击当地
像流水撞击花岗岩。
我看见闪光的声音

镶嵌在你的窗框，

刀叉在油布上，

海豹们的头，突然钻出，

环视万物。

这里的人总相信

溺亡的灵魂寄身海豹。

在朔望潮时可能变形。

它们热爱音乐并游向歌手

歌手可能在夏日将尽时站在

白石灰的储炭棚入口，

他的肩膀倚着门柱，他的歌

是夜晚远海的一叶小舟。

我第一次来时你就唱个不停，

你簸扬的攀升和起奏

让人想起尖镐的采撷。

再高歌吧，老兄。我们依然相信我们听到的。

喉音的缪斯

夏末，午夜时分，
我闻到白天的暑热：
在酒店停车场上方的窗前
我呼吸湖上浑浊的晚风
看一群年轻人离开迪斯科舞厅。

他们的声音升腾，粗重而慰人
如进食的丁鲹在那个黄昏
吐出的油腻泡沫——黏糊的丁鲹
曾被称为"鱼医生"，因为据说
接触它的黏液，鱼的伤口就愈合。

一个穿白色连衣裙的姑娘
在停车场的车辆之间被表白：
当她的声音蜂拥而来，化为欢笑，
我觉得自己像挂满创伤徽章的狗鱼
好想游去接触那轻声软语的生命。

悼念肖恩·奥里亚达[①]

他指挥阿尔斯特管弦乐队
像牧人拿着桦杖
把他们驱向南方。
我从后面观察他,

轻快,身着正装,
一柄黑匕首独特地颤动,
一管翎笔尽情挥舞,
一颗活泼、白发的头颅。

"你怎么工作?
有时我就躺平
像船底的压舱物
聆听布谷。"

船舷竖起的耳朵——
信任这份天赋,

---

① 肖恩·奥里亚达(Sean O'Riada,1941–1971),爱尔兰作曲家。二十世纪六十年代爱尔兰传统音乐复兴运动的核心人物。

不惧天赋的暗流——
如今无人掌舵。

但有一整个下午
船在我俩的体重下沉陷。
我们窘迫地坐在划手座
轮流抛钩或划船

直到成群的鲭鱼从下方游来
宛若魔法召来的随从
乞讨我们的诱饵。
他有着举重若轻的风度，

更像驯鹰人而非渔夫，我想，
摘除怀疑的目光
去迎接鲭鱼条纹的冰凉，
去探听布谷的呼唤。

当他走近并俯向琴键
他是我们的詹姆斯党人，
他是我们年轻的觊觎者
沿着海边行进

饰以慢板和装饰音。

哦，是鲣鸟击打着音阶！

光的米诺鱼。

谐音的滨鸟。

挽　歌

我们活着的方式，
怯懦或勇敢，
都将是我们的生活。
罗伯特·洛威尔，

窗台上的天竺葵
被我书写的台灯照亮，
来自爱尔兰海的风
将它摇晃——

十天前我们还都
坐在这里，和你一起，
挽歌大师，
英语的焊工。

当你主宰着谈话
主宰着你自己的控制
舵柄，嘲笑我
对水的恐惧，

还有什么不在你的皇权之中？

你痛饮美利坚
像喝下"铁
心"伏特加，

宣扬艺术
任性而专横的
爱与傲慢。
你的眼见证你的手

当你英化俄语，
当你逼出
惊心动魄的无韵十四行
表达对哈里雅特①、

莉兹，还有咸咸的
击水的海豚的爱——
你的背鳍
终于擅长

哄骗与击溅，
舵手，织网拆网者，持网的角斗士。
那只手。保护、修饰、
两栖。

---

① 哈里雅特是洛威尔与下一行提及的第二任妻子莉兹的女儿。

凌晨两点，海滨的天气。
不是你伟大诗章的傲帆……
不。你是我们的夜航船
轰鸣在暴风的海上，

这全部技艺回响着
甲胄师的音乐
航道故意穿行
狂放和危险的地带。

此刻大雨如注
天竺葵震颤。
父亲不是孩子的
盾牌——

你发现我身上的孩子
当你与我告别
在成熟的月桂树下
在格兰摩尔门前，

富饶且复元
像那拖延的夏天，
你双眼的鱼跃，
斗胆说出，"我将为你祈祷"。

格兰摩尔十四行诗

给安·萨德尔迈尔
我们最热情的欢迎者

一

元音犁入其他：被开垦的土地。

二十年来最温和的二月

是犁沟上方的雾霭，深沉的无声

不堪远处拖拉机的轰鸣。

我们的路在蒸腾，翻开的土地呼吸。

现在，好日子就是穿过田野，

艺术形如犁铧下的新泥。

我的草地被深深耕耘过。

旧犁铧吞噬每一感官的潜土

我也被一阵馥郁的芬芳唤醒

那根深蒂固的幽暗待放的玫瑰。

啊等等……迎着迷雾，穿着播种者的围裙，

我的幽灵们正阔步踏入春天的驿站。

梦的谷粒如反常的复活节之雪漫天飞旋。

二

隐秘处的探测物、攀爬物，

词语几乎就要进入触觉

从黑暗的铁笼中搜出自己——

"这些事物不是秘密而是谜，"

奥辛·凯利①多年前在贝尔法斯特

告诉我，那时他正在寻找

与刻刀合谋的石头，仿佛纹理

牢记大头锤轻敲而知的事情。

然后我着陆在格兰摩尔的树篱学校，

在沟渠的堤岸上希冀提高

从号角和缓笛捕回的声音，

让它延续、驻留、弥散、平息：

元音犁入其他，被开垦的土地，

每一行诗返回如调转的犁。

---

① 奥辛·凯利（Oisin Kelly，1915–1981），爱尔兰雕塑家。

三

今晚布谷鸟和长脚秧鸡

（这么多，太多了）在暮色中幽会。

一切都是黄昏的抑扬格。

外面的田野上，一只幼兔

认清了它的方向，我也知道鹿群

（从房屋的窗口，我也看到它们，

像行家一样，打探着空气）

在落叶松和五月碧绿的云杉下保持警惕。

我早先说过："我不会从这异乡的孤独中

撤退，既然我把我们带到这里。

多萝西和威廉①——"她打断我：

"你不是要把我俩比作他们吧……？"

屋外一阵轻拂嫩枝的簌簌和风

振奋又平息。是节奏。

---

① 即英国浪漫主义诗人威廉·华兹华斯和妹妹多萝西。他们在
湖区相依为命。

四

我过去常躺下来将耳朵贴近铁轨，

因为，据说，那样会传来一个声音

向前方遁去，一种钢铁的曲调，

是火车轮缘和活塞应和着大地，

但我从未听过。相反，我总听到

两英里外碰撞的车钩和转轨声

飘荡在树林之上。马头

从门前扭转，灰色的后腿和鬃毛

也随之转去，我抬头望向小径，

很快她就会出现在那里。

两方田后，屋里，小小的涟漪

无声地荡漾在我们的饮用水上

（一如此刻它们荡漾在我心上）

后又消融于它们依稀开始的地方。

五

绿荫树①的树干有柔和的皱纹，

它的幼芽新绿，枝条如斑驳的合金：

它是我们童年的荫庇，长大后

一段青翠、潮湿、闪光的记忆。

而且我学会了称它为接骨木。

我爱它开花的样子，像盛满佳肴的浅盘。

它的浆果是黝黑的弹丸鱼子酱，

一串轻盈的卵，一抹淤紫的光。

接骨木？那是梦想着红酒的地方。

绿荫树是有绿荫的树，我曾在树下玩"舔舌头"，

并在我的舌上感到另一条的鲜活质地。

所以，我，根须与嫁接物的词源学家，

返回我的树屋，并将蹲伏在

嫩芽静静抽枝与繁盛的地方。

---

① 原文是"boortree"，来自苏格兰盖尔语，"boor"即"bower"
（树荫），故第 10 行写到"绿荫树"，且它的绿荫是诗人童年游
戏的场所。"boortree"是爱尔兰人（尤其阿尔斯特地区中部）对
接骨木（elderberry）的叫法，"elderberry"是英国的习惯叫法。

六

他住在不可言说的光中。

微雨的正午他看见金钟花，

黄昏，接骨木花如升起的明月，

绿野在晚风吹拂的山坡上暗去。

"我将突破，"他说，"我用完美的

迷雾与和平的缺席制作的釉护层……"

倏然而笃定，像那个挑战坚冰

单车飞越默尤拉河的人。

一个我们从未见过的人。但是，

在一九四七年冬天，当冰雪

使乡间明亮如一间画室，

当寒冷使事物凝结或崩塌，

他的故事让我们复元，天黑后人们

听到一只野雪雁飞过积雪的房屋。

七

多格，罗考尔，马林，爱尔兰海：

碧绿、迅疾的涨潮，北大西洋的涌流

被大风警报的强劲声音召唤而出，

碎成咝咝作响的半影。

午夜与停播。苔原的塞壬，

鳗鱼路、海豹路、龙骨路、鲸鱼路的塞壬

都在羊毛毡背后唱响飓风合成的挽歌，

并将渔船吹送到威克洛的背风处。

"星星号""海雀号""美丽海伦号"

今早在泥泞坎坷的海湾中

照护其明媚的名字。神奇

而真实。我大声说，"避风港"，

这单词变得深邃、明朗，像别处的天空，

在明奇海峡、克罗默蒂港、法罗群岛。

八

雷电在劈开的原木上：大雨点

热如体温并充满不祥

幽暗地溅落于短斧的铁刃。

今早，当一只喜鹊摇摆着

检阅林边露宿的马儿，

我想起盔甲和腐尸上的露珠。

我会遇到什么，血迹斑斑，在路上？

蟾蜍在谷堆里陷得有多深？

是什么穿过漆黑的寂静在庄稼上翻滚？

你还记得朗德的那家客栈吗，

那里一位老妇人摇啊摇啊摇晃

她怀中的痴儿，哼着小曲？

快来我这儿，我正在楼上发抖。

我全部的你，闪电中的白桦林。

九

厨房窗外，一只黑老鼠
在灌木上摇摆像染病的果实：
"它打量我，瞪得我害怕，我不是
在瞎说，你快出去看看。"
难道我们来到乡野就是为此？
我们门前有光彩熠熠的月桂，
古典，挂满隔壁农场传来的
青贮饲料的臭味，腐叶如良知。
血在干草叉上，血在谷壳和干草上，
老鼠在打谷的汗水和尘埃中被刺穿——
我该如何为诗歌辩护？
走下楼，空荡的灌木丛
沙沙作响；远处，你的脸
出没如透过扭曲的玻璃瞥见的新月。

十

我梦见我们睡在多尼戈尔的沼泽，

躺在炭坡，盖着毛毯，我们的脸

彻夜暴露在润湿的细雨中，

苍白如滴水的桦树苗。

寒冷中的洛伦佐和杰茜卡。

待发现的迪尔米德和格兰妮。[①]

黑暗中被施以圣水焚香，我们准备下葬，

宛若加高的土地上呼吸的雕像。

在那梦中我还梦见——你觉得怎样？——

多年前我们在旅店中的第一夜，

你带来预谋已久的吻，

为让我们达成那甜蜜而疼痛的

肉体盟约；我们的独立；

在露湿而迷梦的脸庞中短暂休憩。

---

① 洛伦佐和杰茜卡，莎士比亚《威尼斯商人》中的一对爱人。
迪尔米德和格兰妮是爱尔兰神话中的一对恋人。

九月的歌

在道路的中途
九月末的雨季
白蜡树摇晃，
我们的狗掀开房边的土。

涨水的沟渠里蕨草退去。
浸雨的浆果和石子
又被雨淋，橡果
每日清晨在植草路肩闪烁。

就要结束了，
我们四年的树篱学校生活。
倘若没有人用树脂拂拭琴弓
调试悲伤音域来表现欢乐

我们也会播放旧唱片
听约翰·菲尔德^①的《夜曲》——

---

①约翰·菲尔德（John Field，1782–1837），爱尔兰钢琴家、作曲家，"夜曲"的发明者。他在拜访了圣彼得堡之后，留在那里生活，后来死于莫斯科。

他的天资、荒废、孤寂、声名和欢笑

全都"死在莫斯科",

千般淘洗只为纯净一滴,

音符"如雨滴,天鹅绒上的珍珠"。[1]

还记得我们的美利坚守灵夜吗?[2]

当我们第一次获得自由,

在贝尔法斯特他们掀翻我们的屋顶,

哈蒙德、冈恩和麦克伦

尽情歌唱直到破晓鸟鸣,

漫不经心又心意深重。

狂风,犬吠,电线颤动,

音乐摇摆。屋内屋外,

都是林中婴孩[3]的恶劣天气。我们

在丰茂与光秃的树木间准备服从。

---

[1] 俄罗斯著名音乐家米哈伊尔·伊万诺维奇·格林卡(1804–1857)对约翰·菲尔德的评价。

[2] "美利坚守灵夜"(American wake),这个说法形成于十九世纪初的爱尔兰,当时很多爱尔兰人为摆脱贫困而移民美国,从此一去不返。出发前,人们通常在夜晚至第二天凌晨举行这种类似葬礼守灵的告别仪式,移民者与留守者作最后的告别。传统上,这是一项悲伤的活动。此处指希尼夫妇首次赴美前的情景。

[3] "林中婴孩"(babes-in-the-wood),英国传统童话,讲述两个孩子被弃于森林并死去的故事。常用来比喻天真者陷入危险境地。

身　后

她会把所有诗人打入第九层
让他们互啃头颅，舔舐脑筋；
为惩罚他们生前背后中伤，她让
其地狱成为狂妄自大者的链环。

他们顽固，激烈，雄心勃勃，毫不示弱，
牙关紧闭，如同困兽，人人都像被缚的獾
为抢占有利位置不择手段，互相倾轧
像乌戈利诺骑在大主教罗杰身上。

当她在维吉尔之妻的协助和怂恿下
去巡视那冰封的狱层，
我会大喊，"亲爱的，在我们上界的
绿色大地，是谁戴着月桂，谁的人生

最为尽职且堪称典范？"
她说："我已塞住我媚妇的耳朵
不再听诗人与诗充满硫黄味的消息。
为什么，在我们有生之年，你不能

多放松，笑着从你的房间走下楼来，

黄昏时多与我和孩子们散步——

就像那个有接骨木花和干草的

傍晚，当野蔷薇正在凋零？"

然后（仿佛某个造物者用鱼叉刺我的脖子）

"你不是最糟的。你寻求一种友好，

中立，'双方皆有错'的策略。

你先把我们，再把那些书卷，抛在身后。"

盛 夏

孩子在夜里哭得伤心。

他的卷发长而金黄

邻居们都唤他小不点①

并听他的哭声惊扰夜空

弄湿他们的屋瓦和葡萄藤。

五点钟，房东的拖拉机，

娴熟，无礼，并且卖力，

在院子里奋战，发出隆隆声，

我们享受着百叶窗里的日光

然后睡去。

       沉默负重的河

布满起伏的旋涡

将淤泥和橄榄载入夏天。

燕子从粘在谷仓屋顶的巢中飞出

迷宫般的路线：双重门敞开，

车夫比他佝偻的牛先出来。

我买了纸袋包装的蛆饵，像糖果，

---

① 这里原文为法语"la petite"，阴性，说明邻居把孩子当成
女孩了。

傍晚在泥土的暑热和玉米田

碧绿的臭味中垂钓。

透过草木荫翳的堤岸，如透过交织饰带，

一根根竹竿平静地探出，

点头，等待，试探静谧的触角。

蜗牛在草丛，蝙蝠尖鸣，树木黯淡……

"克里斯托弗在长牙，夜里总哭。

但这谷仓是理想的写作地点：

裸石，旧马具，窗台，货架，干草

和青贮饲料的味道。此刻，一切溽热而寂静。

我花了二十法郎买渔具。"

最后一天，当我收拾东西，

我在温暖的窗台上发现一包蛆

并打开。一群黑压压

活泼泼的东西如从筛漏中落下

仿佛纪录片里失控的警力，

苍蝇如黑子展开轻薄而肥硕的飞翔，

出庭律师和光的黑色贝雷帽。

我们从高处光秃秃的路离开巴斯克

十字架在十字路口站岗如桅杆

那晚就伴着雾中的羊铃入睡。

水　獭

当你扎进水中
托斯卡尼的光波动
漾过整个水池
从水面到水底。

我爱你潮湿的头和激烈的爬泳,
你优美的泳者的肩膀和脊背
不断浮出再浮出水面
今年和今后年年。

我坐在温热的石头上,口干舌燥。
你遥不可及。
这成熟甘美的清澈,这深葡萄色的空气
变得稀薄并令人沮丧。

感谢上帝,为这份慢热,
当我此刻抱着你
我们亲密且深情
像这水上的气氛。

我的双手接通水。
你是我记忆中的水獭
摸得着，软软的，
在此刻的水池，

你转身仰泳，
每一次无声的踢腿
都使光再度倾斜，
为你颈边带来凉意。

然后你突然消失，
又返回，始终专注，
焕新的毛皮笨重而轻快，
在石上留下水印。

臭　鼬

直挺，乌黑，条纹花缎如同
葬礼弥撒上的十字褡，臭鼬的尾巴
炫耀着臭鼬。夜复一夜
我期待她如期待一位访客。

冰箱的嘶鸣渐渐安静。
我台灯的柔光漫出阳台。
小柑橘隐隐地挂在橘树上。
我开始紧张得如一个偷窥者。

十一年后我又开始
写情书，提起"妻子"这个词
像一只陈年的酒桶，仿佛它纤细的元音
已突变成加利福尼亚夜晚的

泥土与空气。美丽、无用的
桉树芳香诉说着你的缺席。
喝下满满一口葡萄酒的后果
就像从冰冷的枕边吸入你。

然后她来了，热切而迷人，
寻常、神秘的臭鼬，
被神秘，祛神秘，
在距我五英尺的地方嗅纸板。

昨晚这一切历历在目，睡前
你的衣服如烟尘飘落撩动我，
你头朝下，翘起屁股在底层抽屉
寻找一件黑色低领睡衣。

回　家

一

为我取那只沙燕来
它掠过并转向
同它自己心贴心
在云端在水面。

二

在磨损的巢穴入口
一次次飞啊飞啊飞翔
它俯冲的羽翼
呵护并亲吻家园。

三

声门无声。耳鼓。
深处，羽毛头①裹紧寂静，
一种河水舐岸的
寂静。

① featherbrain：比喻没头脑的人。

四

让我的肩贴近你。

围拥我。

做噘嘴的湿黏土。

让我在你的屋檐下偷听。

嫉妒之梦

和你及另一位女士散步

在林木葱郁的绿地，低语的青草

用手指抚弄我们猜疑的沉默

而树林敞向一片荫凉、

出人意料的空地，我们坐下来。

我觉得光的坦率令我们沮丧。

我们说起欲望和嫉妒，

我们的交谈是一袭宽松的长裙

或一块白色的野餐桌布

在荒野摊开如一本礼仪书。

"让我看看，"我对我们的同伴说，"我

重涎已久的，你乳房上的淡紫色星星。"

她同意了。哦，无论这些诗句

还是我的慎重，爱人，都无法治愈你受伤的凝视。

围海造田

在突然的发作和局部风暴后
我用双臂将你围绕

并想起这个双脚规环抱
范围之内的部分

荷兰人称为海湾，并用寻①
来称呼展开双臂的距离。

我收回我的围田，
它所有咸涩的青草和泥滑的堤岸；

在深沉的风中，像一株古柳，
我的柳根微微颤动。

①在中古荷兰语里，"bosom"既指"胸部""乳房"，也指"海湾""海面"。"fathom"作名词时，复数指伸开的两臂；单数时指计量单位"寻"，即两臂之间的距离，大约一点八米；作动词时，指"拥抱"，类似英语里的"embrace"。希尼在此展开了词源的想象。

田野工作

一

在山毛榉随着每一缕微风苍白的地方，
在筑巢的乌鸫以完美之眼观察的地方，
在总有一片蕨叶常青的地方

我站在那里凝望你
看你从路口的门房取来软布
伸手去擦拭荆豆上的白石粉。

我能看见你接种疫苗的印痕
在你的上臂拉伸，能闻见煤炭的味道
那是火车从我们之间穿过，一列慢货车，

一节节车厢满载大眼睛的牛。

二

但你的接种疤痕在大腿上，
一个愈合在树皮里的 "O"。

只不过树精不是女人
你是我受伤的树精

散发着母性的气息
如潮湿生癣的栗树。

我们的月亮又小又远，
是久久凝视的硬币

闪耀在 "裴廓德号"① 的桅杆
穿越大西洋和太平洋的水域。

---

① "裴廓德号"（*Pequod*），梅尔维尔经典小说《白鲸》里的捕
鲸船。

三

不是泥潭，
不是杂草丛生的黑水
落满桤木果和带痘痕的叶子。

不是冬日里的牛欧芹
连同它衰朽苍白的胫与膝，
它的嘶音，它的震颤。

甚至也不是夏日浓烈的绿荫
那里蝴蝶纷飞
还有丰满如皮鞍的真菌。

不。而是在一处静谧的角落，
牢牢靠在卵石墙上，
沉甸甸，面朝地，全是嘴巴和眼睛，

向日葵，梦幻的棕黄色。

四

猫尿味儿，
粉红的花开了：
我把一枚
花期的醋栗叶压在
你的手背上
让它缓缓灼烧的
黏稠汁液
为你的皮肤打底，
你的血脉将与
叶脉相互交错。
我舔舔我的大拇指
蘸上一些泥土，
我为被涂油的
叶形涂油。泥土
开花并为你的
手背着色
像一个胎记——
我棕黄的人儿，
你被染污，染污
至完美。

歌

花楸像涂了口红的女孩。
在支路与主路之间
桤木林在潮湿滴沥的远处
兀立于灯芯草丛。

还有讲方言的湿地花朵
还有绝对音高的永生花
还有那一刻鸟儿的歌唱
接近正在发生的音乐。

残　余

一声轻柔的毕剥，日落的烈焰

点燃收割后黑田野里的麦秸，

一场茅草深、焕然一新的

野蛮猩红的燃烧——

我开车驶过英格兰

人们正在烧庄稼

那是庄稼的残余，

被击碎的亚麻色大麦，

从伊里的圣母堂下来，

甜美的男高音拉丁文

被永远废除，

璀璨的彩色窗玻璃

被托马斯·克伦威尔脱粒般脱色。[①]

他现在踏在第几层，

———————

① 圣母堂是伊里大教堂（Ely Cathedral）的一部分，其璀璨的彩色
玻璃窗在一五三六至一五四〇年间的宗教改革运动中被摧毁，替
换为白玻璃，因为清教反对一切形式的宗教装饰。

在圆石上烫伤，

每一颗石子是一尊破损的头像？

午夜之后，夏天之后，

漫步在火星四射的田野，

去闻露水和灰烬的气味

并从滚烫的烟灰召来

威尔·布朗温①的幽魂——

一束穿透的光，

在堆禾束的嗞嗞声

和咔嚓声中游荡。

---

① 威尔·布朗温（Will Brangwen），D.H. 劳伦斯小说《彩虹》中
的人物。

丰收结

当你编织着丰收结
你也将内心醇熟的缄默织入
永不生锈的麦穗
越编越紧也越来越亮
成为一个可知的日冕，
一个廉价的草编同心结。

在梣杖与竹杖上老去的手
一辈子为斗鸡系铁刺的手
听从自身天赋且全神贯注
直到你的手指移动如梦游：
我辨识并触摸它如触盲文，
从可触之物采撷未言之意。

而假若我窥探那金色的草环
我会看到我们走在铁轨的斜坡间
走入那个草长蚊飞的夜晚，
青烟升起，旧苗圃，树丛中的犁，
茅屋外墙贴着拍卖广告——
你的翻领上别着丰收结，

我拿着鱼竿，已开始怀乡

怀念这些夜晚的振奋，当你用手杖

击落野草和灌木的尖梢

不合拍的敲击，敲击，但什么

都没有惊起：那原初的乡土

依然缄默于你手编的草结。

艺术的终极是和平

或可成为这脆弱物件的箴铭

我把它钉在我们的松木橱——

像一个诱捕的圈套

谷神最近从中悄悄溜走

此结却因其穿过而光亮，温暖依旧。

悼念弗朗西斯·莱德威奇[①]

一九一七年七月三十一日在法国遇难

青铜士兵系着一件青铜披风

披风在想象的风中僵硬起皱

不管真实的风怎样扫荡肆虐

他突然俯身的奔跑，永远翘首

眺望佛兰德斯。头盔和背囊，

从枪托到刺刀的坚定角度，

浮雕牌匾上那些忠诚、阵亡的名字——

这一切对于那个不安的小宠儿

一九四六或四七年的我来说不重要，

我紧紧抓住玛丽姑姑的手

沿着斯图尔特港口大道走，绕过新月形街区

穿过城堡小路走向海滨。

来自科尔雷恩的引航员驶向煤船。

恋爱的人们走出中空的沙丘。

---

①弗朗西斯·莱德威奇（Francis Ledwidge，1887–1917），爱尔
兰诗人，死于"一战"。

上身只剩下领扣和反光背心的农民

把裤子撸到他胆怯的小腿。

入夜时彩色灯串点亮海滨

乡音从崖顶的棚舍传来

带来丰产的消息——"我们要把最小的当宠物！"——

而带刺的铁丝网刺伤了弗里斯牛的长辈。

弗朗西斯·莱德威奇，一个星期天的下午

你在德罗赫达远处的海边谈情说爱。

文采飞扬，甜言蜜语，带着乡土气，

你踩着单车穿过斯莱恩的林荫路

你属于那里，那儿忧伤

又美丽：堆满野花的五月圣坛，

复活节的水洒在茅屋，

弥撒石、山顶史前堡垒和椽梁牛棚。

我想起穿英国军装的你，

一张痛苦的天主教徒的脸，苍白而勇敢，

鬼魅般出没于各个战壕，伴着一枝山楂花

或博因河甬道石墓深处的沉寂。

夏天，一九一五年。我看见儿时的

姑妈，正在长长的耕地上放牧。
达达尼尔海峡一处低矮的灌木后
你吮吸石子让你焦渴的口生津。

一九一七年。她依然在放牛
但一阵大规模低空扫射熄灭了伊普尔的烛光：
"我的灵魂在博因河畔，修剪新草坪……
我的祖国穿着她的坚信礼服。"

"被称为英国士兵而我的祖国
在各国之间无法立足……"六周后
你被弹片撕碎。"我很遗憾
党派政治划分了我们的帐篷。"

在你身上，我们死去的谜团，所有旋律
纵横交错为无用的平衡
当风在这警觉的铜像间鸣响
我再度听见那确定而凌乱的鼓点

你追随这鼓声从博因河前往巴尔干
我却想念你的笛子本应吹响的暮音。
你的音调和音高不同于保守党的忠徒
尽管如今你们都在地下合奏。

乌戈利诺

我们已经离开他。我走在冰上

看见两人被焊在一个冰洞

一个压着另一个，一颗头覆盖着另一颗头，

上面的啃咬下面的，后者的颈与头

嫁接在大脑的甜果上，

他啃着就像饥民啃面包。

狂怒的提丢斯也是这样啃食

墨拉尼波斯被割下的头

仿佛啃一颗汁液四溅的肉瓜。

"你，"我大喊道，"上面那个，什么仇恨

让你如此饥饿、无法满足？

什么让你如此狂暴、欲火中烧？

可有什么故事我能替你

讲述，在上方的世界，将他控诉？

如果那时我的舌头还未枯萎在喉中

我将报告真相并澄清你的声名。"

那个罪人松开了他吃食的嘴

来回答我，并用那被他蹂躏的脑袋上

依然生长的头发来抹他的嘴，

然后说，"哪怕我还没开口，

一想到要重温所有那些

绝望的时光就让我心伤；

但既然要哭诉往事，我就要种下

言语的诅咒——使它们在我

啃噬的这颗头上增加并繁殖。

听口音，我知道你来自佛罗伦萨

但我不知道你是谁

也不知你如何来到这下界。

不过，你应该知道我的名字，因为我是

乌戈利诺伯爵，而这个是罗杰大主教，

至于我为什么骑在他身上

这原因当然家喻户晓；我的真诚如何

被他的邪恶轻易伤害，

我如何被抓走、拘留并处死。

但你必须听一听你无法知道的事情

假如你要评判他——我如何

惨死在他手中。所以，听着。

在那座以我命名的"饥饿"监狱

他人也会忧伤，如我曾忧伤；并观望，

如我曾观望，透过狭窄的小孔，

看一个又一个月亮，皓朗，梦游，

从头顶经过，直到那晚我做了

噩梦,于是我未来的面纱也被撕碎。

我看见一次猎狼活动:这人骑马奔驰在

比萨和卢卡之间的山上,纵猎犬去追捕

狼和狼崽。他一派主子威风,

他的猎犬凶猛,他的同伴

部署在他前面,瓜兰迪

和西斯蒙迪也在,还有兰弗兰基,

他们很快就驯服了狼父和狼子

而我的幻觉中

全是尖牙和撕开的流血的肋腹。

当我在黎明前醒来,我的脑袋里

充斥着我儿子们的哭喊声,他们

睡在我身边,泪流满面,哭求面包。

(如果你还没有对我的心

预先遭受的痛苦产生同情,

如果你没有哭泣,那么你就是铁石心肠。)

这时他们醒了,快到往常

食物被送来的时候了,

每个人在梦醒后都神魂不定,

而我听见门被钉死被锤子

封禁,在噩梦般的塔底。

我望着儿子们的脸说不出话。

我的眼睛干涸我的心如石头。

他们哭了，我的小安塞尔姆说，

"怎么了？你为什么这样望着，爸爸？"

但我没有落泪，我没有作答，

整整一天，接下来的整整一夜，

直到又一轮太阳在天空泛红

传来一小束光线来探询这牢狱

四壁内的痛苦。然后当我在

他们的四张脸上看见我的脸

我绝望地咬自己的双手

然后他们，认为是饥饿导致我这样，

突然起身激动地说，

"父亲，如果你把我们吃掉，

这将极大地减轻我们的痛苦，你曾为我们

披上这痛苦的肉身，如今请再为我们脱去。"

于是我镇定自己以便让他们镇定。

我们沉默。那天和下一天悄然流逝

大地似乎对我和他们变得强硬。

整整四天我们任由这沉默积聚。

然后，在我面前平躺下来，

加多说，"你为什么不帮我，父亲？"

他就那样死了，当然如你所见，

我看着三个儿子一个个

在第五天和第六天相继死去

直到我别无所见。摸索，瞎眼，

整整两天我抚摸他们呼喊他们。

悲痛仅使人心伤，而饥饿致命。"

说完这一切，他的眼珠骨碌

他的牙齿，如犬牙咬紧尸骨，

咬入头颅并再度紧紧咬住。

比萨！比萨！你的发音像一阵嘘声

在我国草木繁茂的语言中咝咝作响。

既然邻国在你的终结中

玩忽职守，那就让岛屿

筑起大坝挡住阿尔诺的河口，让

卡普拉亚岛和戈尔戈纳岛筑坝并淹没

你和你的人民。因为出卖

你城堡的乌戈利诺的罪孽，

绝不该由他的儿子们承担。

你的残暴如同忒拜。他们年幼

无辜：休和布里加塔

还有另外两个，他们的名字都在我的歌中。

选自但丁《地狱篇》第三十二和三十三歌

迷失的斯威尼

1983

目录

前　言

　　笔者对《疯癫的斯威尼》(*Buile Suibhne*)的翻译改写主要基于 J.G. 奥基夫的双语版，即爱尔兰文本学会(Irish Text Society)一九一三年版。与此同时，弗兰·奥布莱恩使斯威尼成为小说《双鸟渡》(*At Swim-Two-Birds*)复杂结构的一部分，从而给予主人公第二次生命，忧郁且狂欢；其他许多诗人和学者也一直在译介这部诗歌的不同部分。

　　一九一三年版的基础是一六七一至一六七四年间写于斯莱戈郡的手稿。该手稿是爱尔兰皇家学院斯托藏品(Stowe Collection, Royal Irish Academy)的一部分，奥基夫认为，在语言层面上，"这个文本有可能作于一二〇〇至一五〇〇年间的任何时候"。不过，故事在九世纪已成形。奥基夫援引《艾锡尔书》(*Book of Aicill*)，一部最晚成于十世纪的文本，其中就提到斯威尼发疯的故事和诗歌；其他文学和历史资料中的依据使他得出下面的结论：我们现在看到的《疯癫的斯威尼》是多种传统演化的产物，这些传统可以追溯至莫伊拉战役（公元 637 年）时期，在这场战役中，斯威尼疯了，而且在圣罗南的诅咒下，变成一只空中飞鸟。

于是，我们见到的斯威尼是一种文学创造；不同于芬恩·麦库尔或库丘林，斯威尼不是神话传说中的角色，而是历史人物，尽管我们不确定他是否与历史上一位叫斯威尼的国王有关。但集中在斯威尼这个意象上的文学想象显然受制于新兴的基督教精神与更古老、桀骜的凯尔特气质之间的张力。描写霸道的传教士与神圣国王之间冲突的开头部分，以及结尾在圣默灵修道院（St Moling's Monastery）达成的令人不安的妥协，最明显地呈现了这一反复出现的主题。仅凭这一点就足以使这部作品变得重要，但并未穷尽其全部的重要性。比如说，就斯威尼作为一个被迫流亡、负疚自责、通过言辞表达来宽慰自己的艺术家而言，我们也可将这部作品读作一场发生在自由的创造性想象与宗教、政治、家国义务之间的争吵。在一种更具机会主义的精神下，我们同样可能将斯威尼对西苏格兰和南爱尔兰轻易怀有的文化认同感视为一种范例，供当今阿尔斯特所有的男男女女效仿，或者，思索这个问题：这个爱尔兰虚构故事很有可能是对一个不列颠原型的发展，隐约体现在疯子艾伦的故事中（第46–50部分）。

但这部作品的直接魅力在于其本身打动我们的力量，而不是我们可能在其模式中发现的任何笼统暗示。我们必须去看看《李尔王》，看看埃德加假扮成可怜的汤姆胡言乱语——这本身就是斯威尼境遇的有趣平行——来发现诗歌如何彻底地暴露于自然界的美好与恶劣。我们甚至想回到更久远之前，回到盎格鲁-撒克逊"航海者"的恶劣天气，或者，为了迎合偶尔相反的欢腾心境，回到早期爱尔兰隐士的赞美诗。正是《疯癫的斯威尼》中朴素与坚韧的文风，欢欣与悔恨的复调，最初诱使我想要尝试翻译这部作品，并鼓励我以远非神来之笔的四行诗节持续下去。

我最初的冲动是为了搜寻最佳的抒情瞬间，将它们作为一系列孤立的段落来呈现，独立于故事的语境。这些诗意高度浓烈的时刻，而非叙事的总体结构，确立了这部作品的最高艺术水平，也强烈地吸引着它的译者。但我渐渐感到，我必须承担全作才能赢取翻译这些高光时刻的权利：毕竟，我着手做的，是中世纪文学经典中的力作。

不过，原文中的少量诗节还是被排除在外了（见后文《注释与致谢》）。有时候，我会简写作为衔接的叙事部分，并在有些地方用自由诗去处理那些烈度较高的散文段落。在逐行释义方面，奥基夫始终是我的向导，尽管我偶尔为这些诗赋予一种比爱尔兰原作更加主观的音调。我采用的诗节形式并不反映原文格律的音节与谐音原则，但由于这部作品可被视为抒情文体的入门书——哀歌、对话体、连祷文、吟诵史诗、诅咒——我相信，英语丰富的戏剧性音高能在一定程度上弥补缺失的爱尔兰音律。

然而，我和斯威尼的基本关系是地理意义的。他的王国位于今天的安特里姆郡南部和唐郡北部，而三十多年来我就住在那片地区边上，能看见属于斯威尼的某些地方，其他地方也在听力可及的范围之内——米什山、拉沙金、本尼维纳、敦塞弗里克、班恩河谷、罗伊河、莫恩山。当我开始翻译这部作品时，我刚刚搬到威克洛，离斯威尼最后的安息地圣默灵不远。我住在山林之间，忆起斯威尼所代表的"树篱间的绿魂"最早就体现在补锅匠一家人身上，他们也叫斯威尼，总是露宿沟渠，在我最初上学的路上。不管怎样，他仿佛从一开始就与我同在。

谢默斯·希尼

注释与致谢

文本各部分标以序号，以便与 J.G. 奥基夫爱尔兰文本学会版本的分段一致。

第十六部分删去六个诗节，第四十部分删去七节，第四十三部分删去一节。在第一种情况中，被略去的材料属于历史影射；第二种情形是，晦涩战胜了创意；在第三种情况中，我觉得英语诗结束在倒数第二节的位置效果更好。

第八十二部分，以及第八十三部分的前十五节，也被省略了。这些内容讲述默灵、蒙根和斯威尼之间的对话，基本上是对前面内容的再现，在我看来妨碍了结尾部分的冲力。

我将斯威尼王国的名字达尔阿拉德（Dal Araidhe）英化为达拉里（Dal-Arie），在处理其他地名时遵循了奥基夫注释和索引中的建议。在以下找不到任何帮助信息的情况下，我自行发明了爱尔兰地名的对应名：基尔里根（Kilreagan），克隆基尔（Cloonkill），基尔努（Kilnoo），德拉姆弗里（Drumfree），德拉姆杜夫（Drumduff），基尔苏尼（Kilsooney），杜维（Doovey），克里盖尔

（Creegaille），格拉斯格里（Glasgally）。

感谢戴尔德丽·弗拉纳根、亨利·皮尔逊、柯林·米德尔顿和布伦丹·麦克休教授给予的诸多鼓励和帮助。

迷失的斯威尼

我们已经讲过①，斯威尼——柯尔曼·库尔之子，达拉里的国王——在逃离战争的过程中迷失了。故事交代了斯威尼发病和迷途的缘由，为什么在所有人当中，只有他要承受如此狂乱；也讲述了他此后的遭遇。

1

从前，在爱尔兰，有一个叫罗南·芬恩的人，是一位笃信上帝的尊贵牧师。他苦修，虔诚，是一个积极的传教士，一个真正的基督教战士。他是上帝的好仆人，为了灵魂的好处而惩罚他的肉体，是一面抵御邪恶和魔鬼攻击的盾牌，一个温和、友善、忙碌的人。

2

一次，斯威尼还是达拉里的国王时，罗南在那里给一座名叫基兰尼的教堂划定地界。斯威尼正在一处待着，听到罗南划界的铃声，于是问他的人，这是什么声音。

3

——是罗南·芬恩，比拉赫的儿子，他们说。他正在你的领地给教堂划界，你听到的是他的铃铛叮铃叮铃。

斯威尼勃然大怒，冲到教堂抓牧师。他的

---

① 在中世纪手稿中，这个故事之前是《莫伊拉之战》，其中交代了斯威尼发疯的缘由。

妻子伊欧兰——基恩纳特的康恩的女儿——试图拦住他，伸手去抓他红袍的流苏，但长袍的银扣在肩头崩开，在屋里弹跳起来。她抓住了长袍，但斯威尼却光着身子跑掉了，很快就到了罗南那里。

4　　他发现那牧师正站在一本精美彩绘的诗篇前引吭高歌，赞美天地之主。斯威尼一把夺过书，丢进附近冰冷的湖水深处。书沉入水中，没了踪影。然后他抓住罗南，把他拖出教堂，正在这时，他听见一声警告。警告来自康戈尔·克劳恩的仆人，他带来康戈尔的命令，传唤斯威尼去莫伊拉打仗。他详尽汇报了这次任务的内容，斯威尼立刻跟着仆人走了，留下牧师为失去诗篇而伤心，也为受到如此轻慢和侮辱而恼怒。

5　　一天一夜过去了，一只水獭钻出湖面，把诗篇交还给罗南。诗篇完好无损。罗南为此奇迹感谢上帝，并诅咒斯威尼，说道：

6　　　　　斯威尼擅闯我的地界，
　　　　　严重地侮辱了我，
　　　　　他把强暴的手放在我身上
　　　　　将我拖出基兰尼。

斯威尼听到我的铃，

顿时飞奔而来，

对我狂吼乱叫，

想要搋我赶我。

那般侮辱——被赶出

我划定的土地——

着实难以容忍；

于是上帝应允了我的祈祷。

我的手被斯威尼紧紧攥住

直到他听见一声响亮的命令：

他被召去莫伊拉，受命加入

与唐纳尔的平原大战。

于是我感恩赞叹，

为我得救的恩典，

那不可预料的一丝转机，

来自王子的行军令。

他从远方逼近战场，

这导致他神智迷狂，

他将漫游爱尔兰，疯癫而赤裸，

他将在矛尖上遇见死亡。

他从我这里抢走诗篇，
把它丢进深深的湖水——
上帝将它取回，
一尘不染，毫发无伤。

一天一夜在盈盈的水中，
我斑斓的经书完好无损！
遵从神子的意愿，
一只水獭将它交还。

这部被他亵渎的诗篇
被我加上诅咒之言：
柯尔曼的族类重见诗篇之日
不幸将降临他们头上。

光天化日，光着身子，
斯威尼侵犯我折磨我：
因此，按照上帝的旨意，
斯威尼将永远光身于世。

伊欧兰，基恩纳特的康恩之女，
试图抓住他的长袍拦下他。

伊欧兰为此将得到我的祝福

但斯威尼将活在我的诅咒中。

然后，罗南回到莫伊拉，调解奥德之子唐纳尔 7
与斯坎兰之子康戈尔·克劳恩之间的矛盾，但
没有成功。不过，牧师的出现被视为战争规则
的确认与保证；他们达成协议，除每天开战和
休战之间的时段外，不得进行任何杀戮。然而
斯威尼不断打破牧师批准的每一次和平与休战：
每天白天，在双方交战之前，斯威尼杀死一个
人；每天晚上，在双方休战之后，斯威尼杀死
另一个。然后，在决战之日，斯威尼比任何人
都更早来到战场。

他穿着漂亮的戎装： 8
闪光的丝绸紧贴他的白肤，
织锦腰带绕在身上；
罩衫乃康戈尔所赐，
是对服役和效忠的奖赏，
奢华至极——
颜色猩红，针脚细密，
边缘缀满金银玛瑙，
绶带饰绳沙沙作响，
镶嵌的银钉熠熠发光，

百褶条纹绣着花样。

他双手各持一杆铁矛，

杂色兽角做的盾牌在他背上，

一把金柄宝剑佩在腰间。

9   他快步行进，直到撞见罗南和八个唱赞美诗的
     人。他们为军队祝福，给他们洒圣水，并把剩
     下的水洒在斯威尼身上。斯威尼认为他们这样
     做不过是为了嘲笑他，于是举起一根长矛，猛
     投出去，一下子刺死罗南的一位唱诗人。他又
     朝着牧师本人抛出第二根长矛，刺穿罗南脖子
     上的铃铛，矛杆弹射到空中。罗南爆发了：

10   我的诅咒降临斯威尼

            为他的大不敬。

            他光滑的矛亵渎

            我圣洁的铃，

            摧毁铃中的恩典，

            最初的圣徒曾将它摇响——

            它将诅咒你到树上，

            枝叶间只有鸟的见识。

            正如矛杆折断，

弹到空中；
愿疯癫发作，
袭击你，斯威尼，直到永远。

我的养子被你杀死，
鲜血染红你的矛尖：
为了结这场交易，
你也将死在矛尖下。

倘若欧文忠诚的部落
试图反对我，
乌拉蓝和泰勒
将让他们衰亡。

乌拉蓝和泰勒
已让他们衰亡。
我的诅咒伴随你，
直到时间的终点。

我的祝福属于伊欧兰，
她将繁盛美好，
我的诅咒降临斯威尼，
他的痛苦无期。

11   当集结的军队交锋并像雄鹿那样发出战争的咆
      哮时，我们听到三声巨大的呼喊。斯威尼听到
      这些呼号在游云里回荡，在苍穹里扩音，便抬
      头看，并被一种撕裂一切的黑暗能量占据。

            他的脑筋痉挛，

            他的心智炸裂。

            眩晕，狂躁，摇晃

            和振荡将他席卷，

            他绝望地挣扎、扑打，

            熟悉的地方使他厌恶，

            于是梦想陌生的迁徙。

            他的手指僵硬，

            他的双脚慌张，

            他的心受惊，

            他的感官迷痴，

            他的视线扭曲，

            武器从他手中坠落，

            他以狂乱笨拙的动作升腾，

            仿佛空中飞鸟。

            罗南的诅咒成真。

12   他的脚轻盈地掠过草地，没有碰掉一颗露珠；
      整整一天，他都是一个飞驰的访客，飞过平原

和田野，荒山和沼泽，丛林和湿地；整整一天，没有一处爱尔兰的山坡或山谷、庄园或森林不见他的影迹；然后他抵达阿尔金山谷的比雷格树林，藏在一棵紫杉树中。

那天，奥德之子唐纳尔打了胜仗。斯威尼的一位男性亲戚胖奥格活了下来，和一众人马逃到阿尔金山谷。他们想知道斯威尼的下落，因为战役结束后，他们没见到他的踪影，但他也没被列入亡者当中。他们正合计这个，认为罗南的诅咒与此有关，这时，斯威尼从紫杉树里发出声音：

13

> 战士们，过来。
> 你们来自达拉里，
> 你们要找的人
> 栖在他的树里。

14

> 上帝予我的生命
> 如今赤裸而饥饿；
> 我消瘦憔悴，女人
> 躲避我，音乐也终了。

> 所以我在比雷格树林。

是罗南让我到此地步，

上帝让我自我放逐——

战士们，忘记那个你们认识的人。

15 人们听到斯威尼的吟唱，立刻辨出他，并试图
说服他信任他们。他说永远不会。当他们逼近
那棵树，他敏捷地跃起，飞向蒂尔康诺的基尔
里根，栖息在教堂边的一棵老树上。

　　不料奥德之子唐纳尔和他的军队打完仗后
也来到那里。他们看见这个疯子落在树上，就
包围了树，对着树上的家伙喊出种种猜测；有
人说这是个女人，也有人说这是男的，直到唐
纳尔本人认出他来，说道：

　　——这是斯威尼，达拉里的国王，战役那
天被罗南诅咒。上面的是好人，他说，假如他
需要钱财和补给，他们随时愿意提供，只要他
信任他们。康戈尔的人沦落至此，让我不安，
因为早在我们交战之前，我和他之间就因缘深
厚。但是，当斯威尼同康戈尔一起向苏格兰的
国王借兵和我作战时，他受到了科姆西利的警
告。然后，唐纳尔吟出下面的歌：

16 　　斯威尼，究竟发生了什么？

　　斯威尼，在交战那天的莫伊拉，

你是军队的首领，
也是众人的精英！

曾见你在宴后红了脸，
如金色丰收季的罂粟！
头发像刨花或绒毛，
你天然完美的冠冕。

曾见你英姿飒爽，
在雪后的清晨启程。
你湛蓝晶莹的眼睛
闪亮如风蚀的深冰。

你步伐稳健、优雅，
却跌倒在王权之路，
你是血统纯正的剑客，
敏察机遇并敏锐出击。

科姆西利曾允诺你，好孩子，
允你救赎与王位：
你曾怎样满怀渴望，昂首阔步，
接受天地之音的祝福。

讲真理的预言家科姆西利

在神谕中预告：

所有人都渡海而你在此伫立，

永不从爱尔兰返回。

在莫伊拉的战场

寻找他的谜底，

血滴在明晃的刀尖，

康戈尔在死者之列。

17　斯威尼听到军兵的吵嚷，便从树上腾空，朝着
乌云飞去，在山川与土地上空漫游。

漫长的时间里他遍游爱尔兰，

在坚硬的岩缝探路前行，

挺肩穿过常青藤丛，

在狭窄的山径碰掉落石，

蹚过一个个河口，

攀上一座座顶峰，

涉越一道道丘岭，

直到发现宜人的波凯恩山谷。

那里是天然的避难所，爱尔兰所有的疯子都曾
在那里聚集，度过发疯的年月。

波凯恩山谷是这样的：

它有四个迎风的山口，

美丽的树林，洁净的水井，

清冽的泉水和清澈多沙的溪涧，

碧绿的水田芥和懒散的婆婆纳

缠绵纠结在表面。

它是大自然的贮藏室

藏有酸模，林地酸模，

它的浆果，它的野蒜，

它的黑刺李和它的棕橡果。

疯子们会因为争抢水田芥和岸上的床位而互殴。

斯威尼在那山谷里待了很久，直到一天晚上， 18
他被困在一棵爬满常青藤的山楂树上。他几乎
受不了了，因为每当他辗转反侧，那些带刺的
枝条就会扎到他，让他遍体鳞伤。他换到另一
个地方，来到一丛浓密的荆棘，其中一棵年幼
的黑刺李从多刺的泥床中兀立出来，他便落在
黑刺李的树梢上。但那棵树太纤细了，它摇摇
晃晃，被压弯了腰，斯威尼重重摔在地上，像
一个惨遭屠戮的幸存者。然后他用尽全身力量
爬起来，筋疲力尽，钻出树丛，说道：

——曾经锦衣玉食，今朝苦不堪言。到昨

晚为止，这样的日子已经一年了！

　　然后他吟出这首诗：

19
　　　　　　到昨夜已有一年，
　　　　　　我住在幽暗的枝桠间，
　　　　　　浪迹于潮涨潮落之间，
　　　　　　寒冷而赤裸。

　　　　　　没有枕头可倚靠，
　　　　　　没有人类的陪伴，
　　　　　　救救我吧，上帝，
　　　　　　我没有矛也没有剑。

　　　　　　没有和女人的蜜谈。
　　　　　　相反，我思念
　　　　　　水田芥，思念
　　　　　　洁净的婆婆纳。

　　　　　　没有皇室血液的涌动，
　　　　　　我孤独地在此露营；
　　　　　　没有荣耀点燃树林，
　　　　　　没有朋友，没有音乐。

　　　　　　说真的：命苦啊。

而且无法逃避这宿命；

没有睡眠，没有休息，

也很久没有希望了。

没有嘈杂拥挤的房屋，

没有喧闹善意的人群，

没有人称我国王，

没有美酒和筵席。

如今一道鸿沟裂开，

隔开我和我的随从，

隔开疯狂和理性。

在这山谷间觅食

便是我疯狂的皇室访问：

没有盛大排场或国王巡行，

只有林中狂奔。

天上的圣人啊！神圣的上帝啊！

没有技艺精湛的乐师，

没有柔声细语的女人，

没有敞开手掌的给予；

我注定要漫长地死去。

今晚远非从前，
我的苦难也远远不同，
曾经我用坚定的手掌
统御一方宝地。

我曾飞黄腾达，受到垂青，
勒住强健的坐骑，
策马奔腾，处在
幸运和王权的高潮。

那潮水来了又去，
将我抛在波凯恩山谷，
被废黜，被放逐，
因为我出卖了上帝，

几乎从死神之门坠落，
精疲力竭，遍体鳞伤，
在枝桠坚硬的灌木下，
那褐色多刺的山楂树。

我们的悲伤加倍，
在康戈尔失败的星期二。
我们的亡者如巨大的收成，
我们的残兵是最后一刈野草。

这就是我的苦难。

坠下高贵的峰巅，

悲伤而迷途，

到昨晚已有一年。

他就那样待在波凯恩山谷，直到最后他竭尽全力　　20
飞向班纳与蒂尔康诺交界处的克隆基尔。那天晚
上，他来到井边喝水，吃水田芥，然后就钻进了
教堂边的老树。对斯威尼来说，那晚简直糟透
了。一场可怕的暴风雨来袭，他陷入绝望，说道：

　　——可惜我没有死在莫伊拉，却要忍受如
此苦难。

　　然后他吟出这首诗：

今晚雪好冷。　　　　　　　　　　　21

我已筋疲力尽，

但饥饿和烦恼

没有尽头。

瞧瞧我，残损

而褴褛，

拉沙金的斯威尼。

瞧瞧我现在，

永远在变迁，
开辟新路径，
永远在夜晚。
有时我也怕。

被恐怖占据时
我会起航高飞，
飞过熟知的海域。
我是波凯恩山谷的疯子，

饱经风霜，赤裸
像一棵冬日的树，
披着黝黑的霜
和冰冻的雪。

坚硬的灰树枝
划破我的手，
地上的荆棘
刺伤双脚的皮肤

霜冻的疼痛
让我迷途，
从米什山到加仑山，

从加仑山到库里岛。

在帕特里克山顶
我一路悲啸，
从波凯恩山谷到艾丽岛，
从金蒂岛到莫恩山。

我在黎明醒来
淌着斋戒的口水：
时而在克隆基尔吃水田芥，
时而在基尔努吃碎米荠。

我希望我还在拉沙金
过着安然无恙的生活，
而不是这里，心碎，
赤身，困在雪中。

斯威尼继续走着，直到抵达香农河双鸟渡的教 22
堂，如今叫作克隆布伦的地方；确切地说，他
抵达那天是个星期五。教堂的牧师正在唱申初
经①，女人们在打亚麻，还有一个在分娩。

---

① 天主教七段祈祷时间中的一部分，通常在一天中的"第九
时"，即下午三点整进行。

——这些女人不该违反主的斋戒日规定。那个女人在打亚麻，让我想起我们在莫伊拉挨打。

然后他听见晚祷的钟声响起，说道：

——班恩河畔的布谷啼鸣要比今晚这幽怨的钟声甜美得多。

于是他吟出这首诗：

23

我停下歇息，想象
布谷鸟在河对岸啼鸣，
班恩的布谷，叫声更甜美
胜过幽怨刺耳的教堂钟声。

女人啊，星期五不是
生孩子的好日子，
这一天斯威尼忏悔斋戒
表达对上帝的爱。

不要怀疑我。听着。
在莫伊拉我的部族被打败，
被捶击，被侮辱，被猛攻，
像亚麻被这些女人击打。

从迪奥拉湖畔的险崖
北上德里的科姆西利，

116

我看见大天鹅，听见它们的鸣啭
甜美地斥责战争的烽烟。

在孤寂的绝壁，一头雄鹿的
吼叫让整个山谷激荡
回响。让我沉醉。
超凡的甜美激荡我心。

哦，仁慈清白的上帝，
听我的祈祷，护念我，上帝啊，
让我们永不分离。
让我永远融于你的甜蜜。

第二天，斯威尼来到埃里斯西部的圣德维尔教 24
堂，吃那里的水田芥，饮教堂的水。那夜风雨
大作，想到自己的悲惨处境，他伤心战栗。他
开始想念家乡达拉里，吟出这些诗文：

在德维尔教堂 25
我整夜思念
达拉里，
黑暗中栖居着

上千个鬼魂。

梦复原我：

军队攻击德拉姆弗里，

我进入我的王国，

和我的部队露营，

同法奥楚和康戈尔归来，

在德拉姆杜夫过夜。

那些曾见我在莫伊拉

就范的挑衅者啊，你们

如鬼火挤满我的脑袋，

然后消失，

把我留给黑夜。

26　斯威尼在爱尔兰又流浪了整整七年，直到一个
夜晚，他回到波凯恩山谷。那里是他的方舟和
伊甸园，他在那里隐居，只在恐怖来袭时才会
离开。他在那里过夜，第二天早晨，林奇坎来
寻找他。有人说林奇坎是斯威尼的同父异母兄
弟，也有人说他是领养的兄弟，不管他是谁，
他非常关心斯威尼的情况，三度将他从疯癫中
领回。

　　这一次，林奇坎在山谷中追踪他，在斯威
尼常吃水田芥的小溪边发现了他的脚印。他也

追随落在地上的树枝踪迹，那是斯威尼从一棵树移动到另一棵树时碰掉的。但那天他并没有追上斯威尼，所以他来到山谷间一座废弃的房子里躺了下来，因为一天的追踪和侦查让他疲惫不堪。很快，他就沉沉睡去了。

然后，斯威尼沿着他的跟踪者的足迹，来到这座房前，站在那里听林奇坎的鼾声，吟出这首诗：

我可不敢躺下打鼾 27
呼呼大睡像墙边那男人，
自从莫伊拉一战
我七年没眨过眼。

天主！为什么我在那个
著名的星期二去打仗
却变成疯狂的斯威尼，
孤独地栖身于高高的常青藤？

在克里布的井边，水田芥
是我辰时经①的补给；

————
①辰时经（terce），天主教七段祈祷时间中的第三段，上午九时开始。

那染绿我下巴的汁液
是斯威尼的标志与胎记。

搜捕是一种赎罪。
疯狂的斯威尼在逃亡，
他蜷缩睡在岩壁下
在利格山的阴影中——

长期远离幸福时光，
独自生活，一个光荣的名字；
长期被流放，远离灯芯草的山坡，
远离我芦苇间的家园。

我感恩天上的王，
他的严厉只为证明他的仁爱，
我的冒犯践踏了它，
我的罪过塑造我新的形态——

战栗；闪现于天际，
一个被吓出常青藤的流浪汉。
蜷缩在暴风雨中，
浑身湿透。

虽然我还活着，在紫杉谷

深处出没，爬上高高的山坡，
我愿意跟康戈尔交换场地，
躺在那些死者当中。

我的生命是持续的哀歌。
我头上的屋顶没了。
我注定衣衫褴褛、挨饿发疯，
这一切来自上帝的威力。

想象波凯恩山谷以外的生活
简直令人发疯——
波凯恩山谷，我安枕无忧之地，
我长满苹果树的伊甸园。

墙边那个人，他怎会知道，
斯威尼失败后经历的煎熬？
弓身走过高高的草丛。
饮一口水。吃水田芥。

在白鹭阔步处消夏。
在狼群之中越冬。
在绿了又落了的枝条间梳毛。
墙边那个人，他怎会知道？

我曾经和疯朋友们露宿

波凯恩，快乐的风之谷，

风载着回声，如今生活悲惨，

墙边那个人梦也梦不见。

28 吟罢，第二天夜晚，他来到一座磨坊边。这个磨坊为林奇坎所有。照看磨坊的人是林奇坎的岳母，一位名叫伦农的老太太，是达布·迪特里的女儿。斯威尼进去看她时，她给了他一点吃的，所以，很长一段时间，他不断回到这个磨坊。

一天，当林奇坎外出跟踪斯威尼时，他在磨坊边的小溪旁看见斯威尼，于是过去对那个老太太说了些话。

——斯威尼来过磨坊吗？林奇坎说。

——昨晚他在这里。妇人说。

于是林奇坎假扮成他岳母的样子，在岳母出去后，坐在磨坊里，直到晚上斯威尼回来。但是，斯威尼看到头巾下的眼睛，认出了林奇坎，立刻拔腿就跑，飞出天窗，说道：

——这是可悲的跋涉，林奇坎，你在我喜欢的每一寸爱尔兰土地追踪我。难道你不知道，罗南让我如惊弓之鸟，所以我无法信任你？你这样一直跟着我，让我很生气。

然后他开始赋诗：

林奇坎，你真讨厌。
别缠着我，还我安宁。
罗南对我的诅咒还不够吗
让我过得偷偷摸摸疑神疑鬼？

当我在激烈的战斗中
将致命的长矛抛向罗南，
它劈开他的胸铠，
在牧师铃上留下凹痕。

当我用那绝好的长矛
在战场上击中他，
——就让鸟儿的自由属于你！
是罗南牧师的祈祷。

然后我在他祷告后腾空，
飞升，飞升，飞升，飞在空中，
此后我再没有飞得
那么轻，那么快，那么高。

要回顾那个星期二早晨
光彩夺目的我，且让时间倒流：

我心灵的目光看见自己依然

在列队行军，和我的士兵步调一致。

但如今，我亲眼看见

一件更为惊人的事情：

在一个女人的头巾下，

是林奇坎警觉的眼睛。

30　——你做的一切不过是让我更荒唐，他说。走
吧，别再骚扰我，回你自己的地方去，我也要
去看看我的伊欧兰。

31　斯威尼放弃王位时，他的妻子已经去跟瓜伊尔
住了。有两位男性亲戚对斯威尼放弃的王位拥
有同等的继承权，他们是斯坎兰的两个孙子，
分别叫作瓜伊尔和伊欧柴。当时，伊欧兰和瓜
伊尔在一起，两人穿过菲尤斯林地，前往卡文
的伊甸特里夫狩猎。瓜伊尔的营地就在波凯恩
山谷附近，位于阿马地区的平原上。

　　斯威尼落在伊欧兰小屋的门楣上，对她说道：

　　——夫人，你还记得我们俩在一起时的深情
厚爱吗？对你来说，生活依然快乐，对我却不然。

　　接着，两人开始对话：

斯威尼：

不安如记忆的翅膀

扑闪，我盘旋

在你上方，你的床

还带着你情人的体温。

还记得你曾跟我玩

山盟海誓的游戏吗？

如果你失去你的斯威尼，

日月也将陨落！

但你背信弃义，

践踏誓言如践踏床帏——

不是我晨霜中的床

而是你的、他入侵的床。

伊欧兰：

欢迎你来，我疯狂的爱人，

我最初最后最爱的人！

我现在安逸，但我也曾憔悴，

当我听到你被打败的噩耗。

斯威尼：

你更欢迎那位王子，

他为了你精心打扮，
阔步踏入爱欲的盛筵，
那曾是斯威尼的专享。

伊欧兰：
即便如此，我还是更喜欢
空空的树和光光的斯威尼——
更喜欢昔日我们最甜的游戏——
胜过今朝和他的筵席。

告诉你，斯威尼，即使我得到
尘世和爱尔兰的最佳人选，
我也宁愿跟你走，清白度日，
啜饮清水，吃水田芥。

斯威尼：
但又冷又硬像石头
是斯威尼穿过
利萨道林岩床的路。
我在那里藏身

恐慌，饥饿，赤裸，
一堆皮包骨。
我不再是你的。

你属于另一个男人。

伊欧兰：

我可怜的受苦的疯子！

看见你这样让我很伤心，

你的脸颊苍白，你的皮肤布满伤痕，

荆棘与灌木将它划破。

斯威尼：

但我没有怨言，

我温柔的人儿。

上帝命我受此奴役

让我筋疲力尽。

伊欧兰：

真希望我们能一起飞走，

做流浪的滚石，同羽的飞鸟：

我愿意俯冲伴你欢翔，

在夜晚的巢穴将你抱紧。

斯威尼：

我走南闯北。

一晚我在莫恩山。

也曾远游到班恩河口

和基尔苏尼。

33　　他们话音刚落，军队就从四面八方扫荡了营地。和往常一样，斯威尼仓皇逃离，未敢停歇，直到黄昏来到比雷格树林——他在莫伊拉战役后最初停留的教堂——他又一次钻进教堂的紫杉树里。穆拉·麦克伊尔卡当时是教堂的守门人，他的妻子恰好路过那棵紫杉树，偶然看到那个疯子。她认出了斯威尼，说道：

　　——快从紫杉树上下来，我知道你是达拉里的国王，这里没有别人，只有我，一个女人。

　　她虽这样说，却想要诱骗他进入圈套，把他抓住。

　　——我决不下去，斯威尼说，林奇坎和他的妻子可能突袭我。但如今，要想认出我，岂不是很难？

　　然后他吟出这些诗节：

34　　　　只有你的鹰目
　　　　能将我认出，
　　　　我曾雄踞一方
　　　　在达拉里——

　　　　爱尔兰的谈资

仪表堂堂。

自从战争的冲击

我成了自己的鬼魂。

所以，好女人，看好

你的丈夫和你的屋子。

我不能逗留。审判日那天

我们再相会。

他轻盈地越过树梢，继续赶路，直到抵达拉沙金 35
那棵古树，他在自己国家的三个藏身地之一，另
外两个分别在蒂米尼涅达和克卢安克里玛。在那
棵紫杉树上，他躲藏了六个星期，但最后还是
被发现了，达拉里的贵族们开会决定由谁去逮捕
他。大家一致推选林奇坎，他也同意前往。

　　他来到树下，斯威尼在他头顶的枝上。

　　——真可怜，斯威尼，你竟沦落至此，他
说，像空中任何一只鸟，无食无水无衣，而昔
日你绫罗绸缎，连骑的异域坐骑都披着无与伦
比的马具。你可还记得你的随从，你可爱温柔的
佳人，你的青年才俊和他们的猎犬，那些能工巧
匠？你可还记得你麾下的会众？你可还记得那些
流溢着醉人美酒的酒杯、金樽和兽角？看到你像
可怜的鸟从一处荒地飞到另一处，真让人唏嘘。

——别说了，斯威尼打断他，这是我的命。不过，你有没有来自我的国家的消息？

——我确实有，林奇坎说，你的父亲死了。

——这是个打击，他说。

——你的母亲也死了，年轻人说。

——如今再没人疼我了，他说。

——还有你的兄弟，林奇坎说。

——我的肋在流血，斯威尼说。

——你的女儿也死了，林奇坎说。

——独生女是心头的针，斯威尼说。

——还有你的儿子，曾经唤你"爹爹"，林奇坎说。

——这真是致命一击。他说。

然后，斯威尼和林奇坎互相应和，吟出这首诗：

36   林奇坎：

来自高山的斯威尼，

纯正的剑客，老兵：

为了上帝，你的审判官和救赎者，

说与我，你的养兄弟。

你是否听见我的话，听啊，听啊，

我尊贵的主人，我伟大的王子，
因为我带来，尽量温和地，
关于你家乡的坏消息。

你留下一个死去的王国
正因如此我不得不带来
坏消息：死去的兄弟，
死去的父亲，死去的母亲。

斯威尼：
如果我温柔的母亲死了，
我的流亡更加艰难；
但她对我的爱已冷却
冷却的爱比同情更糟。

那最近丧父的儿子
挣脱羁绊，无拘无束。
他的痛是被坚果压弯的树枝。
死去的兄弟是受伤的肋部。

林奇坎：
众所周知的事情
我还得当新闻告诉你：
尽管你瘦弱，挨饿，你的妻子

思念你而伤心至死。

斯威尼：

一个家若没了妻子，

就像无舵的小船飘摇风雨；

像羽管笔贴紧皮肤；

鳏夫独守他凄清的火炉。

林奇坎：

悲伤积聚心碎，

歌哭弥漫空中。

但这一切就像手握烟云，

既然你还失去了姐妹。

斯威尼：

我无法求助于寻常的智慧

来止住这打击造成的伤口。

姐妹之爱无声无私，

像和煦的阳光照耀沟渠。

林奇坎：

我们的北方如今比过去冷，

牛犊被关在远离母牛的地方，

自从你女儿和你姐姐的儿子，

两个爱你的人，被击倒后。

斯威尼：

我忠实的猎犬，我忠实的外甥——
没有钱财能换取他们对我的爱。
但你拆掉了悲伤的缝线。
心头的针尖是独生女。

林奇坎：

我要告诉你我本不想说的。
它伤到我的痛处！
在达拉里，人人
都在哀悼你死去的儿子。

斯威尼：

这是让众人畏惧的消息。
这是将我们击垮的事情——
损失，记忆的伤口，
那个唤我爹爹的人死了。

这是我无法承受的打击。
抵抗不得不到此为止
你是助猎者，我是鸟儿
受到惊吓从隐蔽处出来。

林奇坎：

斯威尼，现在你在我手里，

告诉你，我能治愈这些伤口。

你家里谁都没有死。

你所有的亲人都活着。

镇静。醒醒。歇歇。

向东回家。忘记西边。

承认吧，斯威尼，你已经

离你牵挂的人太远了。

树木森林和野鹿——

诸如此类更让你快乐

胜过你安稳的东方堡垒

舒适羽绒床上的安睡。

在急流的磨坊水塘边

你栖息的暗绿冬青枝

如今胜过那些

与聪明才俊的宴饮。

山谷里的竖琴音乐

也无法抚慰你：你依然

愿意在橡树上倾听

棕雄鹿对着鹿群发情的叫声。

比山谷中的风更迅捷，

昔日不可一世的斗士，

如今的传奇，狂人——

你的流亡结束了，斯威尼。来！

斯威尼听见独生子的噩耗，从树上栽了下来，37
林奇坎抓住他，给他戴上镣铐。然后，林奇坎
告诉斯威尼，他所有的家人都平安无恙，并护
送他回到达拉里集会的贵族中。他们给斯威尼
戴上枷锁，让他在林奇坎的监视下待了六个星
期。在此期间，贵族们相继拜访斯威尼，最后，
斯威尼终于恢复了理智和记忆，觉得自己又复
原了过去的身形和举止。所以，人们解开他的
锁链，他回到从前的自己，他们的国王。

此后，斯威尼寄宿在林奇坎的卧室里。丰
收的季节到了，一天，林奇坎和他的族人们去
收割庄稼，斯威尼被关在卧室，由磨坊的老太
婆照看，她曾被警告，不准跟斯威尼说话。然
而，她到底还是跟他讲了话，让他聊聊发疯时
的冒险经历。

——斯威尼说，住口，老太婆，你的谈话

太危险。上帝不想让我再疯癫。

——老太婆说，是你对罗南的侮辱让你发了疯。

——斯威尼说，要忍受你的背叛和欺骗实在可厌！

——不是背叛，是实话。

然后，斯威尼说：

38
斯威尼：

老太婆，你从磨坊来到这里

就是为了让我在山林蹦跳？

是不是女人的手段

和背叛让我迷途不返？

老太婆：

斯威尼，你的悲伤众所皆知，

但我不是背叛者：

圣罗南的奇迹

使你成为疯子的一员。

斯威尼：

如果我还是国王，

但愿我再度称王独霸此方，

我不会赐你盛宴和美酒，

老太婆，我会赏你一记耳光。

——听着，女人，他说，要是你知道我经 39
历的磨难。多少次恐怖的跳跃啊，跃过山峦、
堡垒、陆地、山谷。

——看在上帝分上，老太婆说，让我看看
你怎么跳的。让我看看你发疯时的蹦跳。

话音刚落，斯威尼就跃过床栏，落在凳子
的另一端。

——我也能，老太婆说，于是跳了过去。

然后斯威尼又纵身一跳，跳出房屋的天窗。

——我也能，老太婆说着，立刻跳了起来。

无论如何，最后的结局是：那天，斯威尼跃
过达拉里的五个百户区，直到抵达菲盖尔的格林
纳伊塔，老太婆一路紧跟。斯威尼在一簇常青藤
上方小憩，老太婆则栖息在他旁边的树上。

那是丰收季的尾声，斯威尼听到林外人群
中传来一声猎号。

——一定是费莱恩的呐喊，他们要杀了
我，斯威尼说。在莫伊拉，我杀了他们的国王，
这伙人现在来报仇了。

他听见鹿鸣，于是赋诗，盛赞爱尔兰的树
木，也历数自己的磨难和悲伤：

突然间山谷中
传来羊啼和鹿鸣！
那胆小的雄鹿
如受惊的乐手

用思乡恋曲
撩动我心弦——
鹿儿在我迷失的山峦，
羊群遍布平原。

那枝繁叶茂的橡树
在林中最高，
榛树分叉的枝桠
藏起甜美的榛果。

桤木是我的最爱，
峡谷里光滑无刺，
它的汁液里流淌着
某种仁爱之乳。

黑刺李是多刺的鱼篓
装点着黝黑的果实；
在乌鸦饮水的井边
青青的水田芥丛生。

巢菜散布在小路
茎叶里属它最甜；
牡蛎草令我开心
还有那野草莓。

矮胖的苹果树摇动
咚咚落下果实；
山花楸鲜红的浆果
凝成一团如血。

荆棘蜷缩在路边，
拱成一条刺鱼，
吸血并蜷缩成无辜的样子
准备发动下一轮偷袭。

每一座墓园的紫杉
用黑暗的斗篷裹紧夜晚。
常青藤是林中
幽昧的精灵。

冬青竖起它的挡风墙，
一道抵挡冬天的门；
矛杆上的热血

暗淡桦树的纹理。

白桦，光滑而幸福，
微风喜爱的美味，
高枝扎成发辫为你加冕，
树中的女王。

白杨苍白
低语，迟疑：
一千条受惊的短尾
在它的树叶上急摆。

但在这茂密的林中
最让我不安的
是一根来回晃动的
橡树枝。

罗南受到羞辱，
摇响他的教士铃：
我的冲动和盛怒
带来诅咒与奇事。

高贵康戈尔的铠甲，
他的罩衣镶着金边，

用不幸的荣光包裹我
衣褶间充满不祥。

在溃逃的中途
他漂亮的罩衣暴露我，
军队边追边喊：
——抓住那个金袍人！

抓住他，不管是死是活，
人人都行动起来。
撕裂他肢解他，刺他
戳他，没有人会问罪。

骑手们一路追赶
越过唐郡北部，
我敏捷地躲闪背后
投来的每一根标枪。

仿佛我也被
持矛者抛出，高飞，
航线是空中的一声低语，
掠过常青藤的一缕微风。

我赶上受惊的小鹿，

跟随它迅捷的脚步，
抓住它，轻快地骑上它——
一起跃过一座座山巅，

一座座山川，
那是一场纵情狂欢
从伊尼什欧文半岛往南
往南，远达加尔蒂山。

从加尔蒂到利菲
我一路被驱赶着
穿过凄苦的暮色
来到本布尔本的山坡。

那是我漫长无休的
守夜过程的第一晚：
我最后一个安眠之夜，
是与康戈尔作战的前夕。

然后波凯恩山谷便是我的巢，
我的窝我的穴；
我曾攀越那些山坡，
披星戴月。

这心爱的山谷里一间
孤独的茅屋，
给我一座赤色的山峰及其
无垠的旷野，我也不换。

它的水粼粼如露湿的青草，
它的风刺骨，
它高高的婆婆纳，它的水田芥
是最绿的绿色。

我爱那古老的常青树，
叶子苍白的山毛柳，
白桦嘶嘶的旋律，
肃穆的紫杉。

而你，林奇坎，你可以尝试
伪装，欺骗；
在夜晚的面具和披风中到来，
我不会被捉住。

起初，你曾得手，
凭借哀悼逝者的连祷文：
父亲，母亲，女儿，儿子，
兄弟，妻子——你撒谎

但你若还想要发言权，
那么准备好
迎接莫恩的险峰与危崖
以便追踪我。

在常青藤丛，
在虬枝高处，
我会过得很好
且永不复出。

云雀跃起
飞入它们的高空
让我重重跌在
荒野的树墩

而我的匆匆惊动了
斑鸠。
我赶上它，
我全身的羽毛都在狂奔，

然后我又被
受惊的山鹬
或乌鸦突然的鸣啭

所惊动。

想想我的恐慌，
我回到窝里
狐狸正在那儿
啃骨头，

想想我的动荡，
树林中的狼
在前方飞奔
而我腾空飞向山峰，

狐狸的狂吠
在我下方回响，
狼群在我身后
嚎叫撕扯——

它们缥缈的语言，
它们极低的速度，
像噩梦一般
在山脚被甩掉。

如果我逃跑，
我会内疚不安。

我是一只绵羊
没有羊圈

只能在基尔努的
古树里酣眠，
梦回安特里姆与康戈尔
共度的美好时光。

当星耀的寒霜
飘落于水潭
那时我会出现
在无处藏身的山丘：

在寒冷的奈利谷
苍鹭啼鸣，
鸟群迅捷地
来来去去。

我偏爱乌鸦的
匆匆与歌声，
胜过男男女女
寻常的闲谈。

我偏爱獾

在洞穴里长长地尖叫，
胜过清晨狩猎
那一派骚动喧闹。

我偏爱雄鹿
在山巅之间
回肠荡气的求爱声，
胜过那可怕的号角。

那些不羁的奔跑者
纵横山谷！
无人能驯服
高贵的血性，

个个屹立在
各自所有的巅峰，
有角的，警觉的。
想象它们，

高高的费利姆山上的鹿，
莫伊里尼的鹿，
库里的鹿，康希尔的鹿，
布伦双峰上的鹿。

这个兽群的母亲
年迈苍苍，
跟随她的雄鹿们
枝繁，多角。

我愿藏在她头顶
苍苍的密林，
我愿意栖于
她鹿角的迷宫

愿意被高高抛入
鹿角的树丛，
那雄鹿在山谷间
对我呦鸣。

我是斯威尼，抱怨者，
山谷间的疾驰者。
但不如叫我
山脑袋，鹿脑袋。

我始终喜欢的井泉，
一个在丹摩尔，
一个在诺克雷德，
泉水纯净甘冽。

永远的乞丐，
憔悴，匮乏，邋遢，
在群山之巅
像一个饱经风霜的疯哨兵

没有床，没有营舍，
太阳底下无家可归——
甚至在这高高的红红的
羊齿蕨之间也没有。

我唯一的安息：长
眠于神圣的土地，
默灵的泥土为我的伤口
敷上幽暗的油膏。

但此刻山谷间突然传来
羊啼和鹿鸣！
我是胆小的雄鹿
被罗南射中，飘零。

诗罢，斯威尼继续飘零，从菲盖尔，经过班纳 41
格、本尼维纳和麦格拉，始终无法甩掉老太婆，
直到抵达阿尔斯特的敦塞弗里克。在那里，他从

一座堡垒的最高点跃起，跳下一面陡峭的绝壁，诱骗老太婆也跟着跳。她紧跟着他，迅速跳了下去，却摔在敦塞弗里克的峭壁上，粉身碎骨，葬身大海。这就是她跟踪斯威尼的下场。

42　然后斯威尼说：

　　——从现在起，我不会在达拉里逗留，因为林奇坎一定会要我偿命，为老太婆报仇。

　　所以他继续前往康纳特的罗斯考门，落在一座井边，吃那里的水田芥，喝井水。但一个女人走出教堂看守的房子，吓跑了斯威尼，然后这个女人采摘了溪边的水田芥。斯威尼在树上观察她，因为水田芥被她偷走而深深惋惜，他说道：

　　——真遗憾，你拿走我的水田芥。要是你知道我的苦难，知道我众叛亲离，知道我在全世界的山脊都无家可归。水田芥是我的财富，井水是我的美酒，硬邦邦光秃秃的树木和柔软的树荫是我的朋友。就算你不拿那些水田芥，你也不会缺少什么；但你拿走它，就夺去了我的食物。

　　于是赋诗：

43　　　女人啊，你偷走水田芥
　　　又舀走我的水，

你若把这些留给我
也不会更穷。

女人啊，仁慈些！
你我的路不同：
我露宿枝头，
你安居友宅。

女人啊，仁慈些！
想想寒风中的我，
没人记得，没人关心，
没有一件斗篷将我裹紧。

女人啊，倘若你知道
斯威尼已经忘却的悲伤：
长久以来无朋无友，
甚至丧失了友爱的能力。

流亡，被弃，想起
我当国王的日子就觉得可笑，
不再受命统帅军队，
当战士们集结，

不再是爱尔兰

各地的座上宾，
像一个疯癫的朝圣者
浪迹悬崖峭壁。

那弹奏竖琴安抚我的竖琴手，
如今他慰人的音乐在哪里？
还有我的眷属，我的亲友，
他们的温情去哪儿了？

我昔如日中天，鲜衣怒马，
颇有凌云之志：
而今记忆是不驯的烈马
傲立并突然把我抛下。

在星光下的旷野与平原，
女人偷走我的水田芥，
朝着他孤独冰冷的驻地，
斯威尼的影子走去

水田芥是他的畜牧
冷水是他的蜜酒，
灌木作为友伴，
秃山是他的床铺。

拥抱这些，我冰冷的安慰，
永远渴望水田芥，
在艾姆里荒原上
我听见鸿雁的啼鸣，

依然屈服于我的枷锁，
依然是一堆皮包骨，
我摇晃，仿佛遭受了打击
并在苍鹭声中仓皇而去

着陆在达拉里，也许，
在春天，当白昼变换，
却被西垂的暮色再度
惊吓，进入莫恩群山。

凝望下边洁净的砾石，
倾身一方清冽的水井，
饮一口阳光照耀的井水
采一捧水田芥——

就连这些你也要夺走，
微薄的食物稀释我的血
让我在冰冷的高地瑟瑟发抖，
蜷缩在涌起的风中。

早晨的风是最冷的风，
它剥去我的破衣裳，把我冻僵——
记忆让我无语，
女人啊，偷走水田芥。

女人说：
斯威尼，发发慈悲。
把奖惩留给上帝。
不要论断人，免得被论断。
欢欣并祝福。不要苛求。

斯威尼：
那么让我们公平交易，公正合理，
从我紫杉树上的最高法庭：
你若把水田芥留给我，
我就把破衣裳交给你。

没有一处可以安枕。
人类之爱背离我。所以
就让我交换偷芥之罪，
就让你成为替罪羊。

你的贪心让我饥肠辘辘。

因此，就让你从我这里夺走的
也夺走你的好运
让你为爱饥渴。

因为你偷水田芥，你将被
觅食的蓝衫挪威人打劫，
悔恨将吞噬你的心。
真倒霉，我们狭路相逢。

那晚他在罗斯考门过夜，第二天，他来到奥蒂　　44
山，然后是美丽的米什山，接着是布鲁姆山的
高崖，从那里又来到伊尼什姆里。在那之后，
他在一个山洞里待了六个星期。这个洞属于苏
格兰西边艾格岛上的多南。从那里，他继续前
往埃尔萨岩，又待了六个星期，最后离开时，
他跟那里作别，并哀叹自己的处境：

无食无宿，　　　　　　　　　　　45
在冰冻的巢穴
和狂风暴雪中
面对暗日。

被风磨砺的冰。
微弱的阳光投下淡影。

高原孤树上的
一个避难所。

出没鹿径，
忍受风雨，
第一个跨过苍苍
霜草。

我攀向山隘，
雄鹿的鸣叫
响彻山林，
我所到之处

海浪轰鸣，心碎
且疲惫，
尖尾的斯威尼，
咆哮呻吟。

冬夜风萧萧，
我的双脚踩着冰雹
走在莫恩山
斑驳的陡坡

或躺在厄恩湖畔

湿湿的岩床，无眠，
紧张地期盼第一缕光，
然后早早出发。

在敦塞弗里克
轻踏海浪，
在敦罗代尔斯
聆听波涛，

从那个巨浪冲向
另一个奔涌的巨浪
在潮起潮落的巴罗，
一晚在坚硬的敦塞南，

次夜已置身布瓦尼山的
野花之间；
然后是帕特里克
山麓的石枕。

在波洛马平原，
我不停迁徙，
从卢格山
到伯格山。

然后那女人
来捣乱，
搅扰我，
冒犯我，

抢走我
嘴里的食物就跑了。
这是报应，
亘古不变。

我采撷水田芥，
可口又美味，
在波凯恩山谷，
采了四满捧。

我采撷沼泽莓，
稀少又罕见，
还从罗南的井里
喝水。

我的指甲扭曲，
我的腰虚弱，
我的脚流血，
我的腿赤裸——

一群顽固的阿尔斯特人

将从苏格兰

一路追赶

并抓住我。

但沦落得

在此哀歌,

埃尔萨岩。

艰辛的处所!

埃尔萨岩,

海鸥之家,

天知道它是

艰苦的寄居。

埃尔萨岩,

钟形的山,

高达天际,

海的口鼻——

它有坚喙,

我沧桑瘦削:

我俩就像一对

硬腿的仙鹤。

我踩踏岩层的
污水和泡沫，
无人理会，
满心忏悔，

想象远方的
树际线，
层层叠叠抚慰人心
如葱茏的绿雾，

不似莫恩山上
噩梦般漆黑的
湖底和湖面
起伏荡漾。

我需要
树林的安慰，
密斯的某个树丛——
或奥索里的空地。

或是丰收季的阿尔斯特。
斯特朗福，闪着微光。

或者夏日造访

绿色的蒂龙。

在拉马斯我迁徙

到泰尔城的水塘，

途经蜿蜒的香农河

春季的捕鱼。

我常常远及

昔日的领地，

那些训练有素的军队，

那些寸草不生的山坡。

然后斯威尼离开了埃尔萨岩，飞越暴风雨的大   46
海，前往布立吞人的土地。他经过右侧布立吞
人的要塞，发现一片大树林，听见有人在里面
哀哭。有时是痛苦的长啸，有时是疲惫的叹息。
原来这是林中另一个迷途的疯子。斯威尼走近
他。

　　——你是谁啊，朋友？斯威尼问。

　　——一个疯子，他说。

　　——那么，你真是朋友了。我也是疯子。
斯威尼说。你干吗不跟我走呢？

　　——我愿意，那人说，只是我害怕国王或

他的随从抓捕我，我也不确定你是不是跟他们
一伙的。

——我不是，斯威尼说，既然你相信我，
告诉我你叫什么。

——他们叫我"林中人"，那个疯子说。

于是斯威尼吟诗，林中人应和：

47　　　　斯威尼：

怎么了，林中人，

你这般抱怨

蹒跚？为什么

你的头脑错乱？

林中人：

对国王的戒备和恐惧

让我沉默。

我用我舌头的墓石

记录我的故事。

我是林中人。

昔日骁勇

善战。如今藏身

密林。

斯威尼：

我也从林中来。

我是斯威尼，

柯尔曼之子。和你一样，

流亡，迁移。

然后，他们彼此信赖，互诉衷肠。斯威尼对疯　　48
子说：

　　——给我讲讲你的故事。

　　——我是地主的儿子，布立吞疯子说，是
当地人，名叫艾伦。

　　——告诉我，斯威尼问，是什么让你发
疯？

　　——很简单。从前，在这个国家有两个国
王，争夺王位。他们的名字分别是伊欧柴和库
阿古。伊欧柴是更好的国王，我是他的亲戚。
但要通过打仗才能决定谁继承王位。我郑重地
命令首领的每一个族人都穿上银甲。我这样做，
是为了让他们气宇轩昂，在排场和行装上胜过
对方。但是，就因为这个，军人们诅咒我，吼
出三句咒语，让我迷途又恐慌，就成了你看到
的模样。

　　同样，他也问斯威尼是怎么疯的。　　　　49

——罗南的咒语，斯威尼说。在莫伊拉之战，他当众诅咒我，让我腾空而起，飞出战场，从那以后就一直流亡。

——哦，斯威尼，艾伦说，既然我们彼此信赖，从今往后，让我们彼此守护。

　　　　无论谁最先听见
　　　　苍鹭在碧绿的湖边鸣啭
　　　　或鸬鹚清脆的啼鸣
　　　　或者山鹬飞离树枝
　　　　或是鸻鸟惊醒的尖叫
　　　　抑或枯枝上噼噼啪啪的脚步声，
　　　　或者无论谁先看见
　　　　掠过树林的鸟影，
　　　　他必须提醒另一个。
　　　　让我们形影不离
　　　　保持两棵树的距离。
　　　　如果我们中谁先听见这些声音
　　　　或诸如此类的声响，
　　　　就让我们立即逃散。

50　他们就那样过了一年。年底，艾伦对斯威尼说：

——今天，我们必须分开了，因为我生命的尽头到了，我将前往命定之处，迎接我的死。

——你将怎么死呢？斯威尼问。

——很简单，艾伦说。我将前往杜维的瀑布，一阵风将让我失衡坠入飞瀑，于是我就淹死了。然后，我将被葬在一个圣徒的墓园。我将上天堂。现在，斯威尼，告诉我，你的命运会怎样。

斯威尼告诉他接下来的故事，然后他们就分开了。布立吞人走向瀑布，到了那里，淹死了。

然后，斯威尼来到爱尔兰，夜幕降临时，抵达安特里姆的莫伊里尼平原。当他意识到所在之处，他说：

——这里一直是好平原，我曾与一个好人为伴。那是斯坎兰的儿子，我的朋友康戈尔·克劳恩。一天，我在这儿对康戈尔说，我想去投奔另一个主人，因为康戈尔给我的报酬太少了。为了说服我留下来，康戈尔立刻给我一百五十匹骏马，包括他自己的棕色坐骑；还有一百五十柄亮剑，剑上装着獠牙；五十个男仆，五十个女仆；一件用金线锦做的罩衣，还有一条绚丽的真丝格子腰带。

然后斯威尼开始吟诗：

此刻我裸露的皮肤感到

夜晚降临在莫伊里尼，
康戈尔生活过的平原。
此刻在我的回忆里

我看见康戈尔和我
骑马穿过平原，
深入交谈，
前往勒干山。

我对国王说：
——我的服务
没有得到应有的报酬。
我扬言要走。

那么国王做什么了？
他给我上百种
骏马，马具，异国
俘虏，女仆。

还有我的栗色坐骑，
吃得多，跑得快，
他的金线衣，
他的丝腰带。

所以还有哪个平原能跟这个比？

密斯平原可以吗？

或是埃尔基德罗平原

或者布满十字架的莫伊费文？

莫伊朗或莫伊菲，

美丽的康纳特平原，

利菲河岸，班恩山谷，

或者缪尔赫夫纳平原？

我见过所有的平原，

东，南，西，北，

但从没见过哪个

比得上安特里姆的土地。

斯威尼诗罢，继续前往波凯恩山谷，在那里自 53
由自在地游荡，直到遇见一个疯女人。他吓得
赶紧跑开，但直觉认为她也是个痴人，于是他
半路停下，朝她转过身来。不料，她却吓跑了。

　　——啊，上帝啊，人生真是悲惨。斯威尼
说。我被她吓跑，她又被我吓跑。在波凯恩山
谷，避难的胜地！

　　然后他开始吟唱：

谁挑起敌意

谁就不该出生；

愿每个残忍的男女

都不得进天堂之门。

如果三人结党密谋，

总有一个背后中伤或悲叹

如我的悲叹，因为一路上

被荆棘和尖锐的黑刺李刺伤。

起初，疯女人躲开男人。

接着，是更奇怪的一幕：

光着脚，赤着身，

那男人也躲开女人。

十一月，野鸭飞。

从那些漆黑的夜晚到五月

让我们觅食，筑巢，藏身

在常青藤，在褐树林

聆听迟鸟歌声背后

波凯恩山谷的水声，

它的溪流匆匆，静谧，絮语，

还有它河流分岔处的岛屿，

它的榛子树，它的冬青荫，

它的叶子，它的橡果，它的荆棘，

它的坚果，它浓烈的刺李，

它果肉冰凉的冬日浆果：

还有树下，它的猎犬巡行，

它兽角斑驳的雄鹿啼鸣，

它的水不息、不息地瀑流——

波凯恩山谷的水声。

然后，斯威尼走向一座房子，他的妻子伊欧兰
和女仆们住在里面。他站在大门前，对他的前
王后说：

——伊欧兰，你在这儿养尊处优，我却依
然没有一席之地。

——没错，伊欧兰说，但还是进来吧。

——我才不呢，斯威尼说，免得军队把我
困在屋里。

——好吧，女人说，看起来你的脑子还没
好，既然你不想留下来跟我们一起，为什么还
不走开，还我们清净？这里有你清醒时的熟人，
要是他们看到你现在这样，一定很尴尬。

——多糟糕！斯威尼说。现在我算知道了，

相信女人多致命。我对这位不薄。现在她赶我走，要是我当初回来杀死费莱恩的国王奥伊利尔·凯达克，那么现在的贵宾本该是我。

于是他说道：

56
　　任何让女人着迷的男人
　　无论多英俊，都要当心。
　　斯威尼就是活生生的例子，
　　他被他的爱人抛弃了。

　　任何轻信的男人必须
　　警惕她们的背叛：
　　背叛，比如伊欧兰对我，
　　是女人的第二天性。

　　轻信，慷慨，
　　坦率，天真，
　　我赠予马匹和牧群，
　　一天就填满她的草原。

　　在激烈的交战中
　　我足以坚守阵地，
　　当战斗的口号响起，
　　我单手应对三十人。

康戈尔有权要求

战士捍卫阿尔斯特：

——你们之中有谁愿意

迎战费莱恩的国王？

奥伊利尔是个狂暴的巨人，

一手持矛，一手持盾，

昂首阔步，盛气凌人，

不一会儿我们的士兵就被吓退。

但当我留在康戈尔身边说话时

我没有抱怨，也不曾后退：

——虽然奥伊利尔是他们最强大的堡垒，

我会和他血战到底。

我让他短了一个头，

只留下躯干，

鼓舞下又杀死五王子

然后才收手拭剑。

说完，斯威尼悄然升空，轻快地跳过一座座山
峰，一个个丘陵，直到抵达阿尔斯特南部的莫
恩山。他在那儿歇息，说道：

——对于一个疯子来说，此地甚好，但这
里却没有庄稼、牛奶和食物。这个地方虽然壮
美，还是不够舒适、安逸。没有地方可以挡风
遮雨。

　　然后他开始吟唱：

58　　　　　　今晚的莫恩山很冷，
　　　　　　　我的住处荒凉：
　　　　　　　在这风雪交加之地
　　　　　　　没有奶，也没有蜜。

　　　　　　　在枝条锋利的冬青树上
　　　　　　　我颤抖并消瘦，
　　　　　　　严寒刺骨，露宿
　　　　　　　赤裸的山巅。

　　　　　　　潭水结冰，霜在我身上凝固。
　　　　　　　然后我抖落，我挣脱，
　　　　　　　又活过来，像被煽动的余火
　　　　　　　在莱恩斯特向北席卷的风中，

　　　　　　　在万圣前夜和万圣节
　　　　　　　梦秋日的梦，
　　　　　　　念我的故土——

波凯恩山谷的清泉。

不再迷途，无论西东，
暴雪鞭打我裸露的脸，
不再颤抖在某个洞穴，
饥饿、苍白、呓语的狂徒，

而是栖身在斑驳的树荫，
我的停泊处，我冬日的避风港，
我裸石楠中的避难所，
我的皇家城堡，我的国王要塞。

每晚我采集、劫取
并搜刮橡树林。
我的双手深入树叶、树皮
树根和地上被风吹落的果实，

它们搜遍缠结的水田芥，
也摸索沼泽莓，
冰凉的婆婆纳，酸模，湿苔藓，
野蒜和覆盆子，

苹果，榛果，橡果，
尖锐多刺的山楂树上的山楂，

黑莓，飘摇的野草，

橡树林里的全部贮存。

上帝啊，让我待在这儿，

远离旷野和平川。

就让我承受山谷的冰冷。

我害怕冰冷的平原。

59　第二天早上，斯威尼又动身了。他经过莫伊费
文和香农河清澈的绿波；他经过奥蒂山诱人的
缓坡，经过洛克雷铺展的草场，萨克河宜人的
两岸，着陆在辽阔的雷伊湖滨。他在蒂奥布拉
丹的树杈上过夜，那是他最喜欢的藏身处之一，
位于康纳特东部的克里盖尔。

　　巨大的悲伤和苦楚将他笼罩，他说道：

　　——我真是吃尽了苦啊。昨晚的莫恩山很
冷，今晚的蒂奥布拉丹树杈也不会更好。

60　那晚下了雪，雪才落便成冰。于是他说：

　　——自从羽毛从我身上长出，我便吃尽炼
狱之苦。如今仍无片刻缓解。我现在明白了，他
说，即使我注定死去，信任族人好过永远受苦：

61　　　　万能的上帝，我活该受苦，

我割破的脚，我干枯的脸，
饱受风吹雨打，
内心惨淡愁苦。

昨晚我躺在莫恩山，
冷雨飘泼，浑身湿透。
今晚，在痛苦的格拉斯格里，
我被钉在树杈的十字。

我，自从被羽毛囚禁了身躯，
毫不退缩地熬过
无数个长日长夜，
却看不到任何出路。

严酷的天气枯萎我，
冰霜雪雨冰封我。
当我在刺骨的风中畏缩
波凯恩山谷的石楠萦绕我心。

动荡，惊慌，迷途，
我穿越整个国土
从利菲河到班恩下游
从班恩河畔到拉甘两岸；

然后越过拉斯莫尔到罗斯考门，
还有克鲁厄钦周围的农田，
飞过莫伊朗平坦的原野
和菲尤斯灌木丛生的山巅。

或者我前往诺克米尔
山脉的艰难迁徙；
或从格拉斯格里，一场向东的
漫长滑翔，飞往劳斯的山坡。

所有这一切都难以忍受，主啊！
依然无食无宿，
俯身啃食水田芥，
饮河里的冷水。

从秋日的树林中惊起，
被荆豆鞭打，血迹斑斑，
在狼群中狂奔，
同牡赤鹿一起躲闪。

神之子啊，可怜可怜我们！
许久不闻人类的语声！
每晚赤身睡在
最高的树丛，

失去本来的身形和容貌，

群山之巅疯狂的奔跑者，

注定孤独的流浪汉：

神之子啊，可怜可怜我们！

——然而，就算奥德的儿子唐纳尔要杀我，我 62
还是要去达拉里，将命运寄托于族人的慈悲。
若不是那磨坊里的老太婆骗我一阵狂跳，我的
神智本可以足够清醒。

然后，一丝理智的微光重返他身上，他踏上返 63
乡之路，准备在那里安居，将自己托付给族人。

　　罗南听说斯威尼恢复了理智并决定重归故
里，大喊道：

　　——主啊，我恳求您，不要让您的迫害者靠
近教堂，再度骚扰；我恳求您，在他身魂分离、
陷入死亡的长眠之前，不要减轻对他的复仇或缓
解他的痛苦。别忘了，您这是惩一儆百，好让那
些暴君知道，您和您的信众神圣不可侵犯。

上帝满足了他的祷告。当斯威尼出现在菲尤斯 64
高原，他停下来，一动不动：子夜时分，奇怪
的幻象出现在他眼前。血淋淋的无头躯体和没

有躯体的头——五个瘦骨嶙峋、蓄山羊胡的头
颅——尖叫着在路上跳来跳去。当他来到它们
中间，它们正在聊天。

——他是疯子，第一个头说。

——阿尔斯特的疯子，第二个说。

——跟紧他，第三个说。

——愿追踪漫长，第四个说。

——直到他抵达海洋，第五个说。

它们群涌而至，但斯威尼在前方腾空，掠过一
片片树丛；无论山谷多么辽阔，他都能从一边
跳到另一边，从一座山巅跳到另一座山巅。

65　　　　　这些脑袋追赶他，

　　　　　　吐着舌头在狂吠，

　　　　　　又是撕咬又尖叫，

　　　　　　又是哀嚎又长啸。

　　　　　　它们嗅他的小腿和大腿，

　　　　　　它们在他肩头呼吸，

　　　　　　它们用口鼻在他脖后摩擦，

　　　　　　它们撞击树干和岩壁，

　　　　　　它们像瀑布喷发又跌落，

　　　　　　直到他甩掉它们并在

　　　　　　低云的卷舌中逃脱。

他摆脱了它们，山羊头、狗头和他在那儿感见
的所有可怕的家伙。但他此前全部的飘泊和飞
行跟现在的遭遇相比都不值一提，因为他疯
癫发作，一病就是六个星期，直到一天晚上，
他栖息在艾德尼山顶的树梢。清晨，他唱起
哀歌：

> 我的暗夜再度降临。
> 世界前行而我却重返
> 自我的纠缠。我又冻又烧。
> 我是痛苦的裸影。

> 莹莹的霜晶和平滑的冰，
> 鞭打的雪，粗嗓音的风，
> 它们都演绎着我的安魂曲。
> 我的壁炉冷了，我的火熄了。

> 还有谁叫我王子？
> 众王之王，万物之主，
> 废除我的头衔，操纵我的没落，
> 让我因罪而无家可归，妻离子散。

> 为何他在莫伊拉饶我一命？

为何不让我战死沙场？
为何委任磨坊的女巫
做他的天堂之犬和我的复仇女神？

磨坊女巫的磨盘挂在我脖子上！
愿地狱炙烤她的灵魂！她把我拖垮，
让我在煽动下跳跃。
我上了那个老巫婆的当。

然后林奇坎狂吠紧追，
一只穷追不舍的猎犬。
我又因他的谎言而跌落，落入
树下捕捉者的圈套。

他们让我面对丧失的爱。
他们捆住我，把我抬进
屋子。多么荒诞！
我偷听到他们胜利的欢宴

但我渐渐镇定下来，
因为那里有善良的人们，
有嬉戏，还有持续的欢笑。
我的头脑终于恢复了清醒

但很快又瓦解，陷入噩梦。
我又开始新一轮跳高的磨难。
磨坊女巫织她的网，发誓
自己无辜。我因为她才跳

并跃出理智的界限。
她再次向我发起挑战。
我们步调一致像一对韵脚。
我定下步速并开始领舞——

我穿越天窗和屋顶，
我飞过堡垒之外
但她始终紧随。无论坦途歧路
我扬风引领这场追逐。

于是我们走遍爱尔兰。
我是风，她是烟。
我是船首，她是航迹。
我是地球，她是月亮。

但永远都要三思而后跳！
尽管她习惯沼泽和山峦，
敦塞弗里克让她跌了跤。
她跟随我跳下堡垒屋顶

并且像老鹰一样
在空中展开她的肢体。
我原地踏步，看着她
撞击岩石。我很高兴

看见她漂浮的碎片。
群魔拼凑她的尸体
将它埋葬。哦，那收留
她尸骨的土地将被诅咒！

一晚我走过菲尤斯——
山峦漆黑，星光熄灭——
突然间五个割下的头，
五个灯笼鬼，像地狱的蝙蝠，

出现、腾空，将我包围。
然后一个头颅说——又一次受惊！
——这就是阿尔斯特的疯子。
咱们把他赶到海里！

我就像离弦之箭般弹出。
我的双脚离开高原的地面。
山羊头、狗头诅咒我

却不能跟上我。

我活该遭受这一切：
守夜，恐惧，
在水面疾行，
女人痛哭的眼睛。

一次，在他动荡的流亡生涯中，他离开洛克山，　　68
着陆在菲盖尔。他在那里的清溪和树枝间待了
一年，吃红的冬青和棕的橡果，饮菲盖尔河的
水。最后，深深的哀伤笼罩了他，因为他想起
自己不幸的人生，于是吟唱出这首短诗：

　　唉，看看斯威尼现在的样子！　　69
　　他的身体饱受屈辱而变得麻木，
　　无人安慰，无法入睡，
　　独自承受狂风暴雨。

　　我从洛克山来到
　　菲盖尔的边缘，
　　常见的冬青和橡果
　　是我的一日三餐。

　　我在山中待了一整年

忍受我的巨变，

瞄准，瞄准，像一只鸟

盯着冬青果的绯红。

我的悲伤强烈而持久。

今晚我失去了全部力量。

谁还有更多理由哀歌，

除了波凯恩山谷的斯威尼？

70　　一天，斯威尼来到康纳特的拉兰山，在那里偷
偷采集一些水田芥，在一口绿迹斑斑的井边饮
水。一个教士愤愤不平地走出教堂，称呼斯威
尼为吃饱不愁的疯子，责骂蜷缩在紫杉树里的
斯威尼：

71　　　　　教士：

你是不是很满足？

你吃我的水田芥，

又栖息在我小屋旁的

那棵紫杉树上。

　　　　　斯威尼：

哪儿来的"满足"！

我多么恐惧，

多么惊慌，多么害怕，

我连眼都不敢眨。

小小鹌鹑的飞翔

都会让我如此惊慌，敲钟人，

仿佛一大队人马

出来追捕我。

教士，倘若你我

互换位置，想一想：

你会不会享受疯狂？

你会不会感到满足？

斯威尼在康纳特的漫游以蒂拉的阿尔特南告终。　72
这里住着一群虔诚的信徒，是一个美丽的山谷，
一条激流自悬崖冲泻而下，树木在峭壁上开花
结果，还有遮风挡雨的常青藤和枝繁叶茂的果
园，有野鹿、野兔和肥猪；还有皮肤光滑的海
豹，它们从对面的海洋爬上岸，总是睡在悬崖
上。斯威尼强烈渴望拥有这片土地，在诗中高
声赞美它：

阿尔特南的圣崖，　　　　　　　　　　　73

坚果丛，榛树林！

清冽、迅疾的湍流

滚滚冲下峭壁。

常青藤绿而密

橡果尤为珍贵。

挂满果实的枝条

从脑袋沉重的苹果树上点头哈腰。

獾在那里筑洞，

敏捷的野兔在那里安家；

海豹逆流而上，

渡海来到这里。

而在瀑布边，柯尔曼之子，

格什山的罗南的牺牲品，

憔悴、疲惫、饱经风霜的斯威尼，

正睡在树底下。

74   最后，斯威尼来到默灵生活的地方，如今叫
作圣默灵。那时，默灵正专注于圣凯文的《诗
篇》，并且给他的学生们读诗。斯威尼出现在井
边，开始吃水田芥。

    ——你不就是早起的鸟吗？牧师说，并且
接着斯威尼的回答，继续说道：

默灵：　　　　　　　　　　　　　

那么，你要抢占先机咯，

起床、吃饭那么早！

斯威尼：

不是很早，牧师。

罗马已是辰时经。

默灵：

罗马的辰时经，

傻瓜知道什么？

斯威尼：

上帝让我做他的神使，

从日出到日落。

默灵：

那么跟我们说说隐秘的事情，

给我们讲讲上帝的消息。

斯威尼：

我不能。但假如你是默灵，

你自有言说的天赋。

默灵：

你虽然疯，却还机敏。

你怎么认出我的脸我的名？

斯威尼：

在我迷失的日子

我常常休憩在这围地。

默灵：

但是斯威尼，柯尔曼的儿子，

你为何不在一处安顿？

斯威尼：

我偏爱的安息地

是永远平静的生命。

默灵：

愿上帝保佑你。你难道不怕

地狱巨口打滑的边缘？

斯威尼：

我唯一的痛苦是上帝

不许我在地上安息。

默灵：

靠近些。快过来，

想吃什么都随便你。

斯威尼：

牧师，比饥饿更糟的是，

衣不蔽体的痛苦。

默灵：

那么欢迎你穿我的罩衣，

也欢迎你戴我的风帽。

斯威尼：

有时我回忆

不堪回首的往事。

默灵：

你可是斯威尼，莫伊拉之战

逃亡的邪灵？

斯威尼：

我是早起的鸟，

觅食者，如果我是斯威尼。

默灵：

你疯癫、狡猾，知道我的名

认出我面容。怎么做到的？

斯威尼：

多少次逗留于这片围地，

我从空中的藏身处观察你。

默灵：

看看这一页圣凯文的赞美诗

诗篇的纸页已经卷曲。

斯威尼：

在波凯恩山谷深处，

紫杉叶在我的角落卷曲。

默灵：

这片墓园，这全部的色彩斑斓，

难道这里没有你要的欢乐？

斯威尼：

我有别样的欢乐：

是那天莫伊拉的兵众。

默灵：

我将唱弥撒，肃穆

庄重的庆典。

斯威尼：

跃出常青藤

是更高的使命。

默灵：

我的职责唯有苦行，

弱的强的都将我耗尽。

斯威尼：

我的苦行是睡在本尼维纳

冰冷的峭壁。

默灵：

当你命终，是否

死在水畔，还是圣地？

斯威尼：

我将早早逝去。

你的牧人将带来致命伤。

76　——斯威尼，这里欢迎你，默灵说，因为你注定在此生活并死去。你将把你的历险记留给我们，并在此墓园接受基督徒的葬礼。因此，无论你每天在爱尔兰游荡多远，每夜我都使你回到我身边，以便我记录你的经历。

77　这个疯子不断返回默灵，一天去康纳特西部的伊尼什博芬，另一天去美丽的阿萨罗；有些日子，他会瞭望米什山清晰的轮廓，另一些日子，则在莫恩山上瑟瑟发抖。但无论他去哪里，每天晚上他都会回到圣默灵参加晚祷。

　　默灵命他的厨子每天留一些牛奶作为斯威尼的晚餐。厨子名叫缪尔基尔，她的丈夫是默灵的猪倌，名叫蒙根。总之，斯威尼的晚餐是这样的：她把她的脚后跟伸到最近的牛粪里，伸到脚踝那么深，然后在里面灌满新鲜的牛奶。然后，斯威尼会悄悄来到存放牛奶的荒凉角落，把奶舔尽。

78　　一天晚上，缪尔基尔和另一个女人吵了一架，那个女人说：

　　——如果你不喜欢你的丈夫，很遗憾，除了那个你整年见面的疯子，你也别无选择。

猪倌的姐姐恰好在附近偷听，但她什么都没说，等到第二天早晨，她看见缪尔基尔去斯威尼栖身的树篱旁，把牛奶存放在那儿的牛粪里，她就来找弟弟，说道：

——你还是个男人吗？你的妻子正和另一个男人在那树篱里。

嫉妒如风暴，冲昏他的头脑。他愤然起身，从屋内架子上抄起一根长矛，就去找那疯子。斯威尼正在贪婪地喝牛粪坑里的牛奶，半边身子对着猪倌，猪倌就把长矛抛过去，刺中斯威尼左胸的乳头，穿透他的背。

还有一种说法。有人说猪倌在斯威尼喝奶的牛粪里藏了一个鹿角，斯威尼跌进去，撞到鹿角尖而死。

恩纳·迈克布莱肯正在墓园门前敲晨祷的钟，79
看到了发生的一切。他吟出这首诗：

猪倌，这令人难过，这是故意的，　　80
残暴，骇人，罪恶。
无论谁干的，都将活在悔恨中，
因为他杀死了国王，圣徒，神圣的傻瓜。

你指望这样做有什么好处？

你死到临头也没有机会忏悔。

你的灵魂将嚎叫着奔向魔鬼，

你的肉体到最后一息都不被宽恕。

但我期待与他同在天堂，

在一句祈祷文中团聚。

持戒的唱诗班将以赞美诗

祝福真正客人的灵魂。

我为他痛惜心碎。

他出身高贵，颇具威望。

他是国王、疯子。

他的坟墓将使大地神圣。

81　恩纳回去告诉默灵，斯威尼已被他的猪倌蒙根
　　刺杀了。默灵和他的信众立即前往斯威尼躺倒
　　的地方。斯威尼向默灵忏悔，领了圣体，并为
　　此感恩上帝。然后，教士们为他涂油。

83　　　　斯威尼：

　　　　曾经我偏爱

　　　　水边跳跃的斑鸠

　　　　轻柔的欢腾，

　　　　胜过窃窃私语。

曾经我偏爱

山上乌鸫的歌唱

和风雨中的鹿鸣，

胜过这口钟的叮当。

曾经我偏爱

山中松鸡的报晓，

胜过佳人的

嗓音和亲近。

曾经我偏爱

狼群的凄厉嚎叫，

胜过教士用绵羊的怯声

咩咩唱出素歌。

你尽管在你的窝里

纵情豪饮祝酒；

我将用我张开的手掌

从井里蘸水偷喝。

你尽管享受幽居的寂静

与你的信徒交谈；

我将研习波凯恩山谷

猎犬高吠的纯净圣咏。

你尽管在你的宴会厅

享用你的咸肉和鲜肉；

我将住在别处，

因翠绿的水田芥而满足。

猪倌的长矛刺伤我，

利落地穿透我身。

啊，主宰万物的上帝啊，为什么

我没有死在莫伊拉？

在爱尔兰各地

我所有无辜的巢穴，

我记得曾栖息

波凯恩山谷的树林。

上帝啊，我感恩

你的圣餐礼。

无论我曾在世上

犯下何罪，我忏悔。

84   然后，斯威尼的死期来临，默灵在教士们的陪

同下起身，每个人都在斯威尼的墓上放下一枚

石子。

——这里埋葬的人曾被善待，默灵说。那时我们多么欢乐，我们曾沿着这条小路边走边说。我多么喜欢看他在那井边啜饮。现在，这口井就叫"疯人井"，因为他常常在那里饮水、吃水田芥。这口井就以他命名。每一个他常去的地方都将被怀念和珍爱。

然后，默灵说：

我站在斯威尼的墓旁   85
怀念他。他曾喜爱、筑巢、
迁移的每一处地方，
我将永远感到亲切。

因为斯威尼喜爱波凯恩，
我也学会喜爱那里。他将想念
所有跌宕的清溪，
所有长满水田芥的河床。

他总是从那口井饮他的水，
如今我们称之为
疯人井；如今他的名字
始终涌溢于它沙色的清冷。

我等候多时但知道他会来。

我迎接他，待他如上宾。

我用临终圣餐

为他撒上石灰，去见圣灵。

因为疯癫的斯威尼是朝圣者，

拜访每一口井边，

每一条绿色堤岸、水田芥丛生的小溪，

那些水便是他的纪念碑。

现在，如果上帝准许，

起来，斯威尼，握住这引领的手，

它不得不将你放入土中

再拉上大地的黑暗帘幕。

我祈求祝福，在斯威尼的墓旁。

他的回忆涌上我胸膛。

他的灵魂栖在爱之树上。

他的肉体沉入泥土的巢。

86　然后，斯威尼从死亡中升起。默灵领着他，两
人一起朝着教堂的门走去。当他们到门口时，
斯威尼把肩倚在门柱上，发出一声响亮的叹息。
他的灵魂升天，他的肉体被默灵体面地安葬。

这些就是柯尔曼之子、达拉里国王斯威尼的历
险故事。

树上的希尼，哈佛大学，一九九五年
（Joe Wrinn 摄）

Field Work

For Karl and Jane Miller

Contents

Acknowledgements

Acknowledgements are due to the editors of the following where some of these poems appeared for the first time: *Antaeus, Ciphers, Encounter, Honest Ulsterman, The Irish Press, The Irish Times, The Listener, Little Word Machine, Mars, The New Review, The New Yorker, The New York Review of Books, The Paris Review, Poetry Now* (BBC Radio), *Poetry Wales, Prospice, Sewanee Review, Thames Poetry, Threshold* and *The Times Literary Supplement.*

The quotation from Dante, *Purgatorio*, used in *The Strand at Lough Beg*, is taken from the Penguin translation by Dorothy L. Sayers (1955).

Elegy and *Leavings* appeared in a limited edition from Deerfield Press. *Glanmore Sonnets* were published by Charles Seluzicki under the title *Hedge School* (Janus Press).

Oysters

Our shells clacked on the plates.
My tongue was a filling estuary,
My palate hung with starlight:
As I tasted the salty Pleiades
Orion dipped his foot into the water.

Alive and violated
They lay on their beds of ice:
Bivalves: the split bulb
And philandering sigh of ocean.
Millions of them ripped and shucked and scattered.

We had driven to that coast
Through flowers and limestone
And there we were, toasting friendship,
Laying down a perfect memory
In the cool of thatch and crockery.

Over the Alps, packed deep in hay and snow,
The Romans hauled their oysters south to Rome:
I saw damp panniers disgorge
The frond-lipped, brine-stung
Glut of privilege

And was angry that my trust could not repose
In the clear light, like poetry or freedom
Leaning in from sea. I ate the day
Deliberately, that its tang
Might quicken me all into verb, pure verb.

Triptych

I
After a Killing

There they were, as if our memory hatched them,
As if the unquiet founders walked again:
Two young men with rifles on the hill,
Profane and bracing as their instruments.

Who's sorry for our trouble?
Who dreamt that we might dwell among ourselves
In rain and scoured light and wind-dried stones?
Basalt, blood, water, headstones, leeches.

In that neuter original loneliness
From Brandon to Dunseverick
I think of small-eyed survivor flowers,
The pined-for, unmolested orchid.

I see a stone house by a pier.
Elbow room. Broad window light.
The heart lifts. You walk twenty yards
To the boats and buy mackerel.

And today a girl walks in home to us
Carrying a basket full of new potatoes,
Three tight green cabbages, and carrots
With the tops and mould still fresh on them.

II
Sibyl

My tongue moved, a swung relaxing hinge.
I said to her, 'What will become of us?'
And as forgotten water in a well might shake
At an explosion under morning

Or a crack run up a gable,
She began to speak.
'I think our very form is bound to change.
Dogs in a siege. Saurian relapses. Pismires.

Unless forgiveness finds its nerve and voice,
Unless the helmeted and bleeding tree
Can green and open buds like infants' fists
And the fouled magma incubate

Bright nymphs.... My people think money
And talk weather. Oil-rigs lull their future
On single acquisitive stems. Silence
Has shoaled into the trawlers' echo-sounders.

The ground we kept our ear to for so long
Is flayed or calloused, and its entrails
Tented by an impious augury.
Our island is full of comfortless noises.'

III
At the Water's Edge

On Devenish I heard a snipe
And the keeper's recital of elegies
Under the tower. Carved monastic heads
Were crumbling like bread on water.

On Boa the god-eyed, sex-mouthed stone
Socketed between graves, two-faced, trepanned,
Answered my silence with silence.
A stoup for rain water. Anathema.

From a cold hearthstone on Horse Island
I watched the sky beyond the open chimney
And listened to the thick rotations
Of an army helicopter patrolling.

A hammer and a cracked jug full of cobwebs
Lay on the windowsill. Everything in me
Wanted to bow down, to offer up,
To go barefoot, foetal and penitential,

And pray at the water's edge.
How we crept before we walked! I remembered
The helicopter shadowing our march at Newry,
The scared, irrevocable steps.

The Toome Road

One morning early I met armoured cars
In convoy, warbling along on powerful tyres,
All camouflaged with broken alder branches,
And headphoned soldiers standing up in turrets.
How long were they approaching down my roads
As if they owned them? The whole country was sleeping.
I had rights-of-way, fields, cattle in my keeping,
Tractors hitched to buckrakes in open sheds,
Silos, chill gates, wet slates, the greens and reds
Of outhouse roofs. Whom should I run to tell
Among all of those with their back doors on the latch
For the bringer of bad news, that small-hours visitant
Who, by being expected, might be kept distant?
Sowers of seed, erectors of headstones…
O charioteers, above your dormant guns,
It stands here still, stands vibrant as you pass,
The invisible, untoppled omphalos.

A Drink of Water

She came every morning to draw water
Like an old bat staggering up the field:
The pump's whooping cough, the bucket's clatter
And slow diminuendo as it filled,
Announced her. I recall
Her grey apron, the pocked white enamel
Of the brimming bucket, and the treble
Creak of her voice like the pump's handle.
Nights when a full moon lifted past her gable
It fell back through her window and would lie
Into the water set out on the table.
Where I have dipped to drink again, to be
Faithful to the admonishment on her cup,
Remember the Giver fading off the lip.

The Strand at Lough Beg

In Memory of Colum McCartney

> All round this little island, on the strand
> Far down below there, where the breakers strive,
> Grow the tall rushes from the oozy sand.
>
> Dante, *Purgatorio*, I, 100-103

Leaving the white glow of filling stations
And a few lonely streetlamps among fields
You climbed the hills towards Newtownhamilton
Past the Fews Forest, out beneath the stars –
Along that road, a high, bare pilgrim's track
Where Sweeney fled before the bloodied heads,
Goat-beards and dogs' eyes in a demon pack
Blazing out of the ground, snapping and squealing.
What blazed ahead of you? A faked road block?
The red lamp swung, the sudden brakes and stalling
Engine, voices, heads hooded and the cold-nosed gun?
Or in your driving mirror, tailing headlights
That pulled out suddenly and flagged you down
Where you weren't known and far from what you knew:
The lowland clays and waters of Lough Beg,
Church Island's spire, its soft treeline of yew.

There you used hear guns fired behind the house
Long before rising time, when duck shooters
Haunted the marigolds and bulrushes,
But still were scared to find spent cartridges,
Acrid, brassy, genital, ejected,
On your way across the strand to fetch the cows.
For you and yours and yours and mine fought shy,
Spoke an old language of conspirators
And could not crack the whip or seize the day:
Big-voiced scullions, herders, feelers round
Haycocks and hindquarters, talkers in byres,
Slow arbitrators of the burial ground.

Across that strand of yours the cattle graze
Up to their bellies in an early mist
And now they turn their unbewildered gaze
To where we work our way through squeaking sedge
Drowning in dew. Like a dull blade with its edge
Honed bright, Lough Beg half shines under the haze.
I turn because the sweeping of your feet
Has stopped behind me, to find you on your knees
With blood and roadside muck in your hair and eyes,
Then kneel in front of you in brimming grass
And gather up cold handfuls of the dew
To wash you, cousin. I dab you clean with moss
Fine as the drizzle out of a low cloud.
I lift you under the arms and lay you flat.
With rushes that shoot green again, I plait
Green scapulars to wear over your shroud.

A Postcard from North Antrim

In Memory of Sean Armstrong

A lone figure is waving
From the thin line of a bridge
Of ropes and slats, slung
Dangerously out between
The cliff-top and the pillar rock.
A nineteenth-century wind.
Dulse-pickers. Sea campions.

A postcard for you, Sean,
And that's you, swinging alone,
Antic, half-afraid,
In your gallowglass's beard
And swallow-tail of serge:
The Carrick-a-Rede Rope Bridge
Ghost-written on sepia.

Or should it be your houseboat
Ethnically furnished,
Redolent of grass?
Should we discover you
Beside those warm-planked, democratic wharves
Among the twilights and guitars
Of Sausalito?

Drop-out on a come-back,
Prince of no-man's land
With your head in clouds or sand,
You were the clown
Social worker of the town
Until your candid forehead stopped
A pointblank teatime bullet.

Get up from your blood on the floor.
Here's another boat

In grass by the lough shore,
Turf smoke, a wired hen-run –
Your local, hoped for, unfound commune.
Now recite me *William Bloat*,
Sing of *the Calabar*

Or of Henry Joy McCracken
Who kissed his Mary Ann
On the gallows at Cornmarket.
Or Ballycastle Fair.
'Give us the raw bar!'
'Sing it by brute force
If you forget the air.'

Yet something in your voice
Stayed nearly shut.
Your voice was a harassed pulpit
Leading the melody
It kept at bay,
It was independent, rattling, non-transcendent
Ulster – old decency

And Old Bushmills,
Soda farls, strong tea,
New rope, rock salt, kale plants,
Potato-bread and Woodbine.
Wind through the concrete vents
Of a border check-point.
Cold zinc nailed for a peace line.

Fifteen years ago, come this October,
Crowded on your floor,
I got my arm round Marie's shoulder
For the first time.
'Oh, Sir Jasper, do not touch me!'
You roared across at me,
Chorus-leading, splashing out the wine.

Casualty

I

He would drink by himself
And raise a weathered thumb
Towards the high shelf,
Calling another rum
And blackcurrant, without
Having to raise his voice,
Or order a quick stout
By a lifting of the eyes
And a discreet dumb-show
Of pulling off the top;
At closing time would go
In waders and peaked cap
Into the showery dark,
A dole-kept breadwinner
But a natural for work.
I loved his whole manner,
Sure-footed but too sly,
His deadpan sidling tact,
His fisherman's quick eye
And turned observant back.

Incomprehensible
To him, my other life.
Sometimes, on his high stool,
Too busy with his knife
At a tobacco plug
And not meeting my eye,
In the pause after a slug
He mentioned poetry.
We would be on our own
And, always politic
And shy of condescension,
I would manage by some trick

To switch the talk to eels
Or lore of the horse and cart
Or the Provisionals.

But my tentative art
His turned back watches too:
He was blown to bits
Out drinking in a curfew
Others obeyed, three nights
After they shot dead
The thirteen men in Derry.
PARAS THIRTEEN, the walls said,
BOGSIDE NIL. That Wednesday
Everybody held
His breath and trembled.

II

It was a day of cold
Raw silence, wind-blown
Surplice and soutane:
Rained-on, flower-laden
Coffin after coffin
Seemed to float from the door
Of the packed cathedral
Like blossoms on slow water.
The common funeral
Unrolled its swaddling band,
Lapping, tightening
Till we were braced and bound
Like brothers in a ring.

But he would not be held
At home by his own crowd
Whatever threats were phoned,
Whatever black flags waved.
I see him as he turned
In that bombed offending place,

Remorse fused with terror
In his still knowable face,
His cornered outfaced stare
Blinding in the flash.

He had gone miles away
For he drank like a fish
Nightly, naturally
Swimming towards the lure
Of warm lit-up places,
The blurred mesh and murmur
Drifting among glasses
In the gregarious smoke.
How culpable was he
That last night when he broke
Our tribe's complicity?
'Now you're supposed to be
An educated man,'
I hear him say. 'Puzzle me
The right answer to that one.'

III

I missed his funeral,
Those quiet walkers
And sideways talkers
Shoaling out of his lane
To the respectable
Purring of the hearse…
They move in equal pace
With the habitual
Slow consolation
Of a dawdling engine,
The line lifted, hand
Over fist, cold sunshine
On the water, the land
Banked under fog: that morning
I was taken in his boat,

The screw purling, turning
Indolent fathoms white,
I tasted freedom with him.
To get out early, haul
Steadily off the bottom,
Dispraise the catch, and smile
As you find a rhythm
Working you, slow mile by mile,
Into your proper haunt
Somewhere, well out, beyond…

Dawn-sniffing revenant,
Plodder through midnight rain,
Question me again.

The Badgers

When the badger glimmered away
into another garden
you stood, half-lit with whiskey,
sensing you had disturbed
some soft returning.

The murdered dead,
you thought.
But could it not have been
some violent shattered boy
nosing out what got mislaid
between the cradle and the explosion,
evenings when windows stood open
and the compost smoked down the backs?

Visitations are taken for signs.
At a second house I listened
for duntings under the laurels
and heard intimations whispered
about being vaguely honoured.

And to read even by carcasses
the badgers have come back.
One that grew notorious
lay untouched in the roadside.
Last night one had me braking
but more in fear than in honour.

Cool from the sett and redolent
of his runs under the night,
the bogey of fern country
broke cover in me
for what he is:
pig family

and not at all what he's painted.
How perilous is it to choose
not to love the life we're shown?
His sturdy dirty body
and interloping grovel.
The intelligence in his bone.
The unquestionable houseboy's shoulders
that could have been my own.

The Singer's House

When they said *Carrickfergus* I could hear
the frosty echo of saltminers' picks.
I imagined it, chambered and glinting,
a township built of light.

What do we say any more
to conjure the salt of our earth?
So much comes and is gone
that should be crystal and kept

and amicable weathers
that bring up the grain of things,
their tang of season and store,
are all the packing we'll get.

So I say to myself *Gweebarra*
and its music hits off the place
like water hitting off granite.
I see the glittering sound

framed in your window,
knives and forks set on oilcloth,
and the seals' heads, suddenly outlined,
scanning everything.

People here used to believe
that drowned souls lived in the seals.
At spring tides they might change shape.
They loved music and swam in for a singer

who might stand at the end of summer
in the mouth of a whitewashed turf-shed,
his shoulder to the jamb, his song
a rowboat far out in evening.

When I came here first you were always singing,
a hint of the clip of the pick
in your winnowing climb and attack.
Raise it again, man. We still believe what we hear.

The Guttural Muse

Late summer, and at midnight
I smelt the heat of the day:
At my window over the hotel car park
I breathed the muddied night airs off the lake
And watched a young crowd leave the discotheque.

Their voices rose up thick and comforting
As oily bubbles the feeding tench sent up
That evening at dusk – the slimy tench
Once called the 'doctor fish' because his slime
Was said to heal the wounds of fish that touched it.

A girl in a white dress
Was being courted out among the cars:
As her voice swarmed and puddled into laughs
I felt like some old pike all badged with sores
Wanting to swim in touch with soft-mouthed life.

In Memoriam Sean O'Riada

He conducted the Ulster Orchestra
like a drover with an ashplant
herding them south.
I watched him from behind,

springy, formally suited,
a black stiletto trembling in its mark,
a quill flourishing itself,
a quickened, whitened head.

'How do you work?
Sometimes I just lie out
like ballast in the bottom of the boat
listening to the cuckoo.'

The gunwale's lifting ear –
trusting the gift,
risking gift's undertow –
is unmanned now

but one whole afternoon
it was deep in both our weights.
We sat awkward on the thwarts
taking turns to cast or row

until mackerel shoaled from under
like a conjured retinue
fawning upon our lures.
He had the *sprezzatura*,

more falconer than fisherman, I'd say,
unhooding a sceptic eye
to greet the mackerel's barred cold,
to pry whatever the cuckoo called.

As he stepped and stooped to the keyboard
he was our jacobite,
he was our young pretender
who marched along the deep

plumed in slow airs and grace notes.
O gannet smacking through scales!
Minnow of light.
Wader of assonance.

Elegy

The way we are living,
timorous or bold,
will have been our life.
Robert Lowell,

the sill geranium is lit
by the lamp I write by,
a wind from the Irish Sea
is shaking it –

here where we all sat
ten days ago, with you,
the master elegist
and welder of English.

As you swayed the talk
and rode on the swaying tiller
of yourself, ribbing me
about my fear of water,

what was not within your empery?
You drank America
like the heart's
iron vodka,

promulgating art's
deliberate, peremptory
love and arrogance.
Your eyes saw what your hand did

as you Englished Russian,
as you bullied out
heart-hammering blank sonnets
of love for Harriet

and Lizzie, and the briny
water-breaking dolphin –
your dorsal nib
gifted at last

to inveigle and to plash,
helmsman, netsman, *retiarius*.
That hand. Warding and grooming
and amphibious.

Two a.m., seaboard weather.
Not the proud sail of your great verse…
No. You were our night ferry
thudding in a big sea,

the whole craft ringing
with an armourer's music
the course set wilfully across
the ungovernable and dangerous.

And now a teem of rain
and the geranium *tremens*.
*A father's no shield
for his child –*

you found the child in me
when you took farewells
under the full bay tree
by the gate in Glanmore,

opulent and restorative
as that lingering summertime,
the fish-dart of your eyes
risking, 'I'll pray for you.'

Glanmore Sonnets

for Ann Saddlemeyer
our heartiest welcomer

I

Vowels ploughed into other: opened ground.
The mildest February for twenty years
Is mist bands over furrows, a deep no sound
Vulnerable to distant gargling tractors.
Our road is steaming, the turned-up acres breathe.
Now the good life could be to cross a field
And art a paradigm of earth new from the lathe
Of ploughs. My lea is deeply tilled.
Old ploughsocks gorge the subsoil of each sense
And I am quickened with redolence
Of the fundamental dark unblown rose.
Wait then... Breasting the mist, in sowers' aprons,
My ghosts come striding into their spring stations.
The dream grain whirls like freakish Easter snows.

II

Sensings, mountings from the hiding places,
Words entering almost the sense of touch
Ferreting themselves out of their dark hutch –
'These things are not secrets but mysteries,'
Oisin Kelly told me years ago
In Belfast, hankering after stone
That connived with the chisel, as if the grain
Remembered what the mallet tapped to know.
Then I landed in the hedge-school of Glanmore
And from the backs of ditches hoped to raise
A voice caught back off slug-horn and slow chanter
That might continue, hold, dispel, appease:
Vowels ploughed into other, opened ground,
Each verse returning like the plough turned round.

III

This evening the cuckoo and the corncrake
(So much, too much) consorted at twilight.
It was all crepuscular and iambic.
Out on the field a baby rabbit
Took his bearings, and I knew the deer
(I've seen them too from the window of the house,
Like connoisseurs, inquisitive of air)
Were careful under larch and May-green spruce.
I had said earlier, 'I won't relapse
From this strange loneliness I've brought us to.
Dorothy and William –' She interrupts:
'You're not going to compare us two…?'
Outside a rustling and twig-combing breeze
Refreshes and relents. Is cadences.

IV

I used to lie with an ear to the line
For that way, they said, there should come a sound
Escaping ahead, an iron tune
Of flange and piston pitched along the ground,
But I never heard that. Always, instead,
Struck couplings and shuntings two miles away
Lifted over the woods. The head
Of a horse swirled back from a gate, a grey
Turnover of haunch and mane, and I'd look
Up to the cutting where she'd soon appear.
Two fields back, in the house, small ripples shook
Silently across our drinking water
(As they are shaking now across my heart)
And vanished into where they seemed to start.

V

Soft corrugations in the boortree's trunk,
Its green young shoots, its rods like freckled solder:
It was our bower as children, a greenish, dank
And snapping memory as I get older.
And elderberry I have learned to call it.
I love its blooms like saucers brimmed with meal,
Its berries a swart caviar of shot,
A buoyant spawn, a light bruised out of purple.
Elderberry? It is shires dreaming wine.
Boortree is bower tree, where I played 'touching tongues'
And felt another's texture quick on mine.
So, etymologist of roots and graftings,
I fall back to my tree-house and would crouch
Where small buds shoot and flourish in the hush.

VI

He lived there in the unsayable lights.
He saw the fuchsia in a drizzling noon,
The elderflower at dusk like a risen moon
And green fields greying on the windswept heights.
'I will break through,' he said, 'what I glazed over
With perfect mist and peaceful absences....'
Sudden and sure as the man who dared the ice
And raced his bike across the Moyola River.
A man we never saw. But in that winter
Of nineteen forty-seven, when the snow
Kept the country bright as a studio,
In a cold where things might crystallize or founder,
His story quickened us, a wild white goose
Heard after dark above the drifted house.

VII

Dogger, Rockall, Malin, Irish Sea:
Green, swift upsurges, North Atlantic flux
Conjured by that strong gale-warning voice
Collapse into a sibilant penumbra.
Midnight and closedown. Sirens of the tundra,
Of eel-road, seal-road, keel-road, whale-road, raise
Their wind-compounded keen behind the baize
And drive the trawlers to the lee of Wicklow.
L'Etoile, Le Guillemot, La Belle Hélène
Nursed their bright names this morning in the bay
That toiled like mortar. It was marvellous
And actual, I said out loud, 'A haven,'
The word deepening, clearing, like the sky
Elsewhere on Minches, Cromarty, The Faroes.

VIII

Thunderlight on the split logs: big raindrops
At body heat and lush with omen
Spattering dark on the hatchet iron.
This morning when a magpie with jerky steps
Inspected a horse asleep beside the wood
I thought of dew on armour and carrion.
What would I meet, blood-boltered, on the road?
How deep into the woodpile sat the toad?
What welters through this dark hush on the crops?
Do you remember that pension in *Les Landes*
Where the old one rocked and rocked and rocked
A mongol in her lap, to little songs?
Come to me quick, I am upstairs shaking.
My all of you birchwood in lightning.

IX

Outside the kitchen window a black rat
Sways on the briar like infected fruit:
'It looked me through, it stared me out, I'm not
Imagining things. Go you out to it.'
Did we come to the wilderness for this?
We have our burnished bay tree at the gate,
Classical, hung with the reek of silage
From the next farm, tart-leafed as inwit.
Blood on a pitch-fork, blood on chaff and hay,
Rats speared in the sweat and dust of threshing –
What is my apology for poetry?
The empty briar is swishing
When I come down, and beyond, your face
Haunts like a new moon glimpsed through tangled glass.

X

I dreamt we slept in a moss in Donegal
On turf banks under blankets, with our faces
Exposed all night in a wetting drizzle,
Pallid as the dripping sapling birches.
Lorenzo and Jessica in a cold climate.
Diarmuid and Grainne waiting to be found.
Darkly asperged and censed, we were laid out
Like breathing effigies on a raised ground.
And in that dream I dreamt – how like you this? –
Our first night years ago in that hotel
When you came with your deliberate kiss
To raise us towards the lovely and painful
Covenants of flesh; our separateness;
The respite in our dewy dreaming faces.

September Song

In the middle of the way
under the wet of late September
the ash tree flails,
our dog is tearing earth beside the house.

In rising ditches the fern subsides.
Rain-logged berries and stones
are rained upon, acorns
shine from grassy verges every morning.

And it's nearly over,
our four years in the hedge-school.
If nobody is going to resin a bow
and test the grieving registers for joy

we might as well put on our old record
of John Field's *Nocturnes* –
his gifts, waste, solitude, reputation, laughter,
all 'Dead in Moscow',

all those gallons of wash for the pure drop,
notes 'like raindrops, pearls on velvet.'
Remember our American wake?
When we first got footloose

they lifted the roof for us in Belfast,
Hammond, Gunn and McAloon
in full cry till the dawn chorus,
insouciant and purposeful.

Gusts, barking, power-lines shaken
and the music wavering. Inside and out,
babes-in-the-wood weather. We toe the line
between the tree in leaf and the bare tree.

An Afterwards

She would plunge all poets in the ninth circle
And fix them, tooth in skull, tonguing for brain;
For backbiting in life she'd make their hell
A rabid egotistical daisy-chain.

Unyielding, spurred, ambitious, unblunted,
Lockjawed, mantrapped, each a fastened badger
Jockeying for position, hasped and mounted
Like Ugolino on Archbishop Roger.

And when she'd make her circuit of the ice,
Aided and abetted by Virgil's wife,
I would cry out, 'My sweet, who wears the bays
In our green land above, whose is the life

Most dedicated and exemplary?'
And she: 'I have closed my widowed ears
To the sulphurous news of poets and poetry.
Why could you not have, oftener, in our years

Unclenched, and come down laughing from your room
And walked the twilight with me and your children –
Like that one evening of elder bloom
And hay, when the wild roses were fading?'

And (as some maker gaffs me in the neck)
'You weren't the worst. You aspired to a kind,
Indifferent, faults-on-both-sides tact.
You left us first, and then those books, behind.'

High Summer

The child cried inconsolably at night.
Because his curls were long and fair
the neighbours called him *la petite*
and listened to him harrowing the air
that damped their roof-tiles and their vines.
At five o'clock, when the landlord's tractor,
familiar, ignorant and hard,
battled and gargled in the yard,
we relished daylight in the shutter
and fell asleep.
                Slubbed with eddies,
the laden silent river
ran mud and olive into summer.
Swallows mazed from nests caked up on roof-tiles
in the barn: the double doors stood open,
the carter passed ahead of his bowed oxen.

I bought the maggots in paper bags, like sweets,
and fished at evening in the earthy heat
and green reek of the maize.
From that screened bank, as from a plaited frieze,
bamboo rods stuck leniently out,
nodding and waiting, feelers into quiet.
Snails in the grass, bat-squeak, the darkening trees....

'Christopher is teething and cries at night.
But this barn is an ideal place to write:
bare stone, old harness, ledges, shelves, the smell
of hay and silage. Just now, all's hot and still.
I've scattered twenty francs on fishing tackle.'

On the last day, when I was clearing up,
on a warm ledge I found a bag of maggots
and opened it. A black

and throbbing swarm came riddling out
like newsreel of a police force run amok,
sunspotting flies in gauzy meaty flight,
the barristers and black bérets of light.

We left by the high bare roads of the *pays basque*
where calvaries sentry the crossroads like masts
and slept that night near goatbells in the mists.

The Otter

When you plunged
The light of Tuscany wavered
And swung through the pool
From top to bottom.

I loved your wet head and smashing crawl,
Your fine swimmer's back and shoulders
Surfacing and surfacing again
This year and every year since.

I sat dry-throated on the warm stones.
You were beyond me.
The mellowed clarities, the grape-deep air
Thinned and disappointed.

Thank God for the slow loadening,
When I hold you now
We are close and deep
As the atmosphere on water.

My two hands are plumbed water.
You are my palpable, lithe
Otter of memory
In the pool of the moment,

Turning to swim on your back,
Each silent, thigh-shaking kick
Re-tilting the light,
Heaving the cool at your neck.

And suddenly you're out,
Back again, intent as ever,
Heavy and frisky in your freshened pelt,
Printing the stones.

The Skunk

Up, black, striped and damasked like the chasuble
At a funeral mass, the skunk's tail
Paraded the skunk. Night after night
I expected her like a visitor.

The refrigerator whinnied into silence.
My desk light softened beyond the verandah.
Small oranges loomed in the orange tree.
I began to be tense as a voyeur.

After eleven years I was composing
Love-letters again, broaching the word 'wife'
Like a stored cask, as if its slender vowel
Had mutated into the night earth and air

Of California. The beautiful, useless
Tang of eucalyptus spelt your absence.
The aftermath of a mouthful of wine
Was like inhaling you off a cold pillow.

And there she was, the intent and glamorous,
Ordinary, mysterious skunk,
Mythologized, demythologized,
Snuffing the boards five feet beyond me.

It all came back to me last night, stirred
By the sootfall of your things at bedtime,
Your head-down, tail-up hunt in a bottom drawer
For the black plunge-line nightdress.

Homecomings

Fetch me the sandmartin
skimming and veering
breast to breast with himself
in the clouds in the river.

II

At the worn mouth of the hole
flight after flight after flight
the swoop of his wings
gloved and kissed home.

III

A glottal stillness. An eardrum.
Far in, featherbrains tucked in silence,
a silence of water
lipping the bank.

IV

Mould my shoulders inward to you.
Occlude me.
Be damp clay pouting.
Let me listen under your eaves.

A Dream of Jealousy

Walking with you and another lady
In wooded parkland, the whispering grass
Ran its fingers through our guessing silence
And the trees opened into a shady
Unexpected clearing where we sat down.
I think the candour of the light dismayed us.
We talked about desire and being jealous,
Our conversation a loose single gown
Or a white picnic tablecloth spread out
Like a book of manners in the wilderness.
'Show me,' I said to our companion, 'what
I have much coveted, your breast's mauve star.'
And she consented. O neither these verses
Nor my prudence, love, can heal your wounded stare.

Polder

After the sudden outburst and the squalls
I hooped you with my arms

and remembered that what could be contained
inside this caliper embrace

the Dutch called *bosom*; and *fathom*
what the extended arms took in.

I have reclaimed my polder,
all its salty grass and mud-slick banks;

under fathoms of air, like an old willow
I stir a little on my creel of roots.

Field Work

Where the sally tree went pale in every breeze,
where the perfect eye of the nesting blackbird watched,
where one fern was always green

I was standing watching you
take the pad from the gatehouse at the crossing
and reach to lift a white wash off the whins.

I could see the vaccination mark
stretched on your upper arm, and smell the coal smell
of the train that comes between us, a slow goods,

waggon after waggon full of big-eyed cattle.

II

But your vaccination mark is on your thigh,
an O that's healed into the bark.

Except a dryad's not a woman
you are my wounded dryad

in a mothering smell of wet
and ring-wormed chestnuts.

Our moon was small and far,
was a coin long gazed at

brilliant on the *Pequod*'s mast
across Atlantic and Pacific waters.

III

Not the mud slick,
not the black weedy water
full of alder cones and pock-marked leaves.

Not the cow parsley in winter
with its old whitened shins and wrists,
its sibilance, its shaking.

Not even the tart green shade of summer
thick with butterflies
and fungus plump as a leather saddle.

No. But in a still corner,
braced to its pebble-dashed wall,
heavy, earth-drawn, all mouth and eye,

the sunflower, dreaming umber.

Catspiss smell,
the pink bloom open:
I press a leaf
of the flowering currant
on the back of your hand
for the tight slow burn
of its sticky juice
to prime your skin,
and your veins to be crossed
criss-cross with leaf-veins.
I lick my thumb
and dip it in mould,
I anoint the anointed
leaf-shape. Mould
blooms and pigments
the back of your hand
like a birthmark –
my umber one,
you are stained, stained
to perfection.

Song

A rowan like a lipsticked girl.
Between the by-road and the main road
Alder trees at a wet and dripping distance
Stand off among the rushes.

There are the mud-flowers of dialect
And the immortelles of perfect pitch
And that moment when the bird sings very close
To the music of what happens.

Leavings

A soft whoosh, the sunset blaze
of straw on blackened stubble,
a thatch-deep, freshening
barbarous crimson burn –

I rode down England
as they fired the crop
that was the leavings of a crop,
the smashed tow-coloured barley,

down from Ely's Lady Chapel,
the sweet tenor latin
forever banished,
the sumptuous windows

threshed clear by Thomas Cromwell.
Which circle does he tread,
scalding on cobbles,
each one a broken statue's head?

After midnight, after summer,
to walk on a sparking field,
to smell dew and ashes
and start Will Brangwen's ghost

from the hot soot –
a breaking sheaf of light,
abroad in the hiss
and clash of stooking.

The Harvest Bow

As you plaited the harvest bow
You implicated the mellowed silence in you
In wheat that does not rust
But brightens as it tightens twist by twist
Into a knowable corona,
A throwaway love-knot of straw.

Hands that aged round ashplants and cane sticks
And lapped the spurs on a lifetime of game cocks
Harked to their gift and worked with fine intent
Until your fingers moved somnambulant:
I tell and finger it like braille,
Gleaning the unsaid off the palpable,

And if I spy into its golden loops
I see us walk between the railway slopes
Into an evening of long grass and midges,
Blue smoke straight up, old beds and ploughs in hedges,
An auction notice on an outhouse wall –
You with a harvest bow in your lapel,

Me with the fishing rod, already homesick
For the big lift of these evenings, as your stick
Whacking the tips off weeds and bushes
Beats out of time, and beats, but flushes
Nothing: that original townland
Still tongue-tied in the straw tied by your hand.

The end of art is peace
Could be the motto of this frail device
That I have pinned up on our deal dresser –
Like a drawn snare
Slipped lately by the spirit of the corn
Yet burnished by its passage, and still warm.

In Memoriam Francis Ledwidge

Killed in France 31 July 1917

The bronze soldier hitches a bronze cape
That crumples stiffly in imagined wind
No matter how the real winds buff and sweep
His sudden hunkering run, forever craned

Over Flanders. Helmet and haversack,
The gun's firm slope from butt to bayonet,
The loyal, fallen names on the embossed plaque –
It all meant little to the worried pet

I was in nineteen forty-six or seven,
Gripping my Aunt Mary by the hand
Along the Portstewart prom, then round the crescent
To thread the Castle Walk out to the strand.

The pilot from Coleraine sailed to the coal-boat.
Courting couples rose out of the scooped dunes.
A farmer stripped to his studs and shiny waistcoat
Rolled the trousers down on his timid shins.

At night when coloured bulbs strung out the sea-front
Country voices rose from a cliff-top shelter
With news of a great litter – 'We'll pet the runt!' –
And barbed wire that had torn a friesian's elder.

Francis Ledwidge, you courted at the seaside
Beyond Drogheda one Sunday afternoon.
Literary, sweet-talking, countrified,
You pedalled out the leafy road from Slane

Where you belonged, among the dolorous
And lovely: the May altar of wild flowers,
Easter water sprinkled in outhouses,
Mass-rocks and hill-top raths and raftered byres.

I think of you in your Tommy's uniform,
A haunted Catholic face, pallid and brave,
Ghosting the trenches with a bloom of hawthorn
Or silence cored from a Boyne passage-grave.

It's summer, nineteen-fifteen. I see the girl
My aunt was then, herding on the long acre.
Behind a low bush in the Dardanelles
You suck stones to make your dry mouth water.

It's nineteen-seventeen. She still herds cows
But a big strafe puts the candles out in Ypres:
'My soul is by the Boyne, cutting new meadows....
My country wears her confirmation dress.'

'To be called a British soldier while my country
Has no place among nations....' You were rent
By shrapnel six weeks later. 'I am sorry
That party politics should divide our tents.'

In you, our dead enigma, all the strains
Criss-cross in useless equilibrium
And as the wind tunes through this vigilant bronze
I hear again the sure confusing drum

You followed from Boyne water to the Balkans
But miss the twilit note your flute should sound.
You were not keyed or pitched like these true-blue ones
Though all of you consort now underground.

Ugolino

(*from* Dante, *Inferno*, xxxii, xxxiii)

We had already left him. I walked the ice
And saw two soldered in a frozen hole
On top of other, one's skull capping the other's,
Gnawing at him where the neck and head
Are grafted to the sweet fruit of the brain,
Like a famine victim at a loaf of bread.
So the berserk Tydeus gnashed and fed
Upon the severed head of Menalippus
As if it were some spattered carnal melon.
'You,' I shouted, 'you on top, what hate
Makes you so ravenous and insatiable?
What keeps you so monstrously at rut?
Is there any story I can tell
For you, in the world above, against him?
If my tongue by then's not withered in my throat
I will report the truth and clear your name.'

That sinner eased his mouth up off his meal
To answer me, and wiped it with the hair
Left growing on his victim's ravaged skull,
Then said, 'Even before I speak
The thought of having to relive all that
Desperate time makes my heart sick;
Yet while I weep to say them, I would sow
My words like curses – that they might increase
And multiply upon this head I gnaw.
I know you come from Florence by your accent
But I have no idea who you are
Nor how you ever managed your descent.
Still, you should know my name, for I was Count
Ugolino, this was Archbishop Roger,
And why I act the jockey to his mount
Is surely common knowledge; how my good faith
Was easy prey to his malignancy,

How I was taken, held, and put to death.
But you must hear something you cannot know
If you're to judge him – the cruelty
Of my death at his hands. So listen now.

Others will pine as I pined in that jail
Which is called Hunger after me, and watch
As I watched through a narrow hole
Moon after moon, bright and somnambulant,
Pass overhead, until that night I dreamt
The bad dream and my future's veil was rent.
I saw a wolf-hunt: this man rode the hill
Between Pisa and Lucca, hounding down
The wolf and wolf-cubs. He was lordly and masterful,
His pack in keen condition, his company
Deployed ahead of him, Gualandi
And Sismundi as well, and Lanfranchi,
Who soon wore down wolf-father and wolf-sons
And my hallucination
Was all sharp teeth and bleeding flanks ripped open.
When I awoke before the dawn, my head
Swam with cries of my sons who slept in tears
Beside me there, crying out for bread.
(If your sympathy has not already started
At all that my heart was foresuffering
And if you are not crying, you are hardhearted.)

They were awake now, it was near the time
For food to be brought in as usual,
Each one of them disturbed after his dream,
When I heard the door being nailed and hammered
Shut, far down in the nightmare tower.
I stared in my sons' faces and spoke no word.
My eyes were dry and my heart was stony.
They cried and my little Anselm said,
"What's wrong? Why are you staring, daddy?"
But I shed no tears, I made no reply
All through that day, all through the night that followed

Until another sun blushed in the sky
And sent a small beam probing the distress
Inside those prison walls. Then when I saw
The image of my face in their four faces
I bit on my two hands in desperation
And they, since they thought hunger drove me to it,
Rose up suddenly in agitation
Saying, "Father, it will greatly ease our pain
If you eat us instead, and you who dressed us
In this sad flesh undress us here again."
So then I calmed myself to keep them calm.
We hushed. That day and the next stole past us
And earth seemed hardened against me and them.
For four days we let the silence gather.
Then, throwing himself flat in front of me,
Gaddo said, "Why don't you help me, father?"
He died like that, and surely as you see
Me here, one by one I saw my three
Drop dead during the fifth day and the sixth day
Until I saw no more. Searching, blinded,
For two days I groped over them and called them.
Then hunger killed where grief had only wounded.'
When he had said all this, his eyes rolled
And his teeth, like a dog's teeth clamping round a bone,
Bit into the skull and again took hold.

Pisa! Pisa, your sounds are like a hiss
Sizzling in our country's grassy language.
And since the neighbour states have been remiss
In your extermination, let a huge
Dyke of islands bar the Arno's mouth, let
Capraia and Gorgona dam and deluge
You and your population. For the sins
Of Ugolino, who betrayed your forts,
Should never have been visited on his sons.
Your atrocity was Theban. They were young
And innocent: Hugh and Brigata
And the other two whose names are in my song.

Sweeney Astray

Contents

Introduction

This version of *Buile Suibhne* is based on J. G. O'Keeffe's bilingual edition, which was published by the Irish Texts Society in 1913. In the meantime, Flann O'Brien gave its central character a second life, as hilarious as it was melancholy, when he made Sweeney part of the apparatus of his novel *At Swim-Two-Birds*; and a number of other poets and scholars have continued to make translations of different sections of the verse.

The basis of the 1913 edition is a manuscript written in County Sligo between 1671 and 1674. This manuscript is part of the Stowe collection in the Royal Irish Academy and O'Keeffe believed that, on linguistic grounds, 'the text might have been composed at any time between the years 1200 and 1500.' Nevertheless, the thing was already taking shape in the ninth century. O'Keeffe cites a reference in the *Book of Aicill*, a text dating from the tenth century at the latest, to stories and poems relating to Sweeney's madness; and other evidence from literary and historical sources leads him to conclude that the *Buile Suibhne* which we now possess is a development of traditions dating back to the time of the Battle of Moira (AD 637), the battle where Sweeney went mad and was transformed, in fulfilment of St Ronan's curse, into a bird of the air.

What we have, then, is a literary creation; unlike Finn McCool or Cuchulain, Sweeney is not a given figure of myth or legend but an historically situated character, although the question of whether he is based upon an historical king called Sweeney has to remain an open one. But the literary imagination which fastened upon him as an image was clearly in the grip of a tension between the newly dominant Christian ethos and the older, recalcitrant Celtic temperament. The opening sections which recount the collision between the peremptory ecclesiastic and the sacral king, and the closing pages of uneasy reconciliation set in St. Moling's monastery, are the most explicit treatment of this recurrent theme. This alone makes the work a significant one, but it does not exhaust its significance. For example, insofar as Sweeney is also a figure of the artist, displaced, guilty, assuaging himself by his utterance, it is possible to read the work as an aspect of the quarrel between free creative imagination and the constraints of religious, political, and domestic obligation. It is equally possible, in a more opportunistic spirit, to dwell upon Sweeney's easy sense of cultural affinity with both western Scotland and southern Ireland as exemplary for all men and women in contemporary Ulster, or to ponder the thought that the Irish invention may well have been a development of a British original, vestigially present in the tale of the madman called Alan (Sections 46–50).

But the work makes its immediate claims more by its local power to affect us than by any general implications we may discover in its pattern. We have to go to *King Lear*, to Edgar's jabbering masquerade as poor Tom – itself an interesting parallel to Sweeney's condition – to find poetry as piercingly exposed to the beauties and severities of the natural world. We may even want to go back further, to the hard weather of the Anglo-Saxon "Seafarer," or, in order to match the occasional opposite moods of jubilation, to the praise poetry of the early Irish hermits. It was the bareness and durability of the writing in *Buile Suibhne*, its double note of relish and penitence, that first tempted me to try my hand at translating and gave me the encouragement to persist with stretches of less purely inspired quatrains.

My first impulse had been to forage for the best lyric moments and to present them as a series of orphaned passages, out of the context of the story. These points of poetic intensity, rather than the overall organization of the narrative, establish the work's highest artistic levels and offer the strongest invitations to the translator of verse. Yet I gradually felt I had to earn the right to do the high points by undertaking the whole thing: what I was dealing with, after all, is a major work in the canon of medieval literature.

Nevertheless, a small number of the original stanzas have been excluded (see Notes, page 271). I have occasionally abbreviated the linking narrative and in places have used free verse to render the more heightened prose passages. O'Keeffe has been my guide to the interpretation of the line-by-line meaning, though I have now and again invested the poems with a more subjective tone than they possess in Irish. The stanza forms employed do not reflect the syllabic and assonantal disciplines of the original metres, but since the work could be regarded as a primer of lyric genres – laments, dialogues, litanies, rhapsodies, curses – I trust that the variety of dramatic pitch in the English will compensate to some extent for the loss of the metrical satisfactions in the Irish.

My fundamental relation with Sweeney, however, is topographical. His kingdom lay in what is now south County Antrim and north County Down, and for over thirty years I lived on the verges of that territory, in sight of some of Sweeney's places and in earshot of others – Slemish, Rasharkin, Benevenagh, Dunseverick, the Bann, the Roe, the Mournes. When I began work on this version, I had just moved to Wicklow, not all that far from Sweeney's final resting ground at St. Mullins. I was in a country of woods and hills and remembered that the green spirit of the hedges embodied in Sweeney had first been embodied for me in the persons of a family of tinkers, also called Sweeney, who used to camp in the ditchbacks along the road to the first school I attended. One way or another, he seemed to have been with me from the start.

S. H.

Notes and Acknowledgements

The sections of the text are numbered to correspond with J. G. O'Keeffe's divisions in the Irish Texts Society edition.

Six stanzas have been dropped from Section 16, seven from Section 40, and one from Section 43. In the first case, the material omitted is historical allusion; in the second, obscurity defeated ingenuity; and in the third, I felt that the English poem came to rest better at the penultimate stanza.

Section 82 and the first fifteen stanzas of Section 83 have also been excluded. There an exchange occurs between Moling, Mongan, and Sweeney which is essentially a recapitulation and seemed to me to impede the momentum of the conclusion.

I have anglicized the name of Sweeney's kingdom, Dal Araidhe, to Dal-Arie, and in dealing with other place names have followed the suggestions in O'Keeffe's notes and index. In the following cases, where no help was offered, I took the liberty of inventing my own equivalents of the Irish: Kilreagan, Cloonkill, Kilnoo, Drumfree, Drumduff, Kilsooney, Doovey, Creegaille, Glasgally.

I am grateful for various encouragements and assistances offered by Dr. Deirdre Flanagan, Henry Pearson, Colin Middleton, and Professor Brendan McHugh.

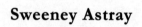

Sweeney Astray

We have already told how Sweeney, son of Colman   1
Cuar and king of Dal-Arie, went astray when he
flew out of the battle. This story tells the why and
the wherefore of his fits and trips, why he of all men
was subject to such frenzies; and it also tells what
happened to him afterwards.

There was a certain Ronan Finn in Ireland, a holy   2
and distinguished cleric. He was ascetic and pious, an
active missionary, a real Christian soldier. He was a
worthy servant of God, one who punished his body
for the good of his soul, a shield against vice and the
devil's attacks, a gentle, genial, busy man.

One time when Sweeney was king of Dal-Arie,   3
Ronan was there marking out a church called
Killaney. Sweeney was in a place where he heard the
clink of Ronan's bell as he was marking out the site,
so he asked his people what the sound was.
  – It is Ronan Finn, son of Bearach, they said. He is
marking out a church in your territory and what you
hear is the ringing of his bell.
  Sweeney was suddenly angered and rushed away
to hunt the cleric from the church. Eorann, his wife,
a daughter of Conn of Ciannacht, tried to hold him
back and snatched at the fringe of his crimson cloak,
but the silver cloak-fastener broke at the shoulder and
sprang across the room. She got the cloak all right but
Sweeney had bolted, stark naked, and soon landed
with Ronan.

He found the cleric glorifying the King of heaven and   4
earth, in full voice in front of his psalter, a beautiful
illuminated book. Sweeney grabbed the book and
flung it into the cold depths of a lake nearby, where it
sank without trace. Then he took hold of Ronan and
was dragging him out through the church when he
heard a cry of alarm. The call came from a servant

of Congal Claon's who had come with orders from
Congal to summon Sweeney to battle at Moira.
He gave a full report of the business and Sweeney
went off directly with the servant, leaving the cleric
distressed at the loss of his psalter and smarting from
such contempt and abuse.

5   A day and a night passed and then an otter rose out
of the lake with the psalter and brought it to Ronan,
completely unharmed. Ronan gave thanks to God for
that miracle, and cursed Sweeney, saying:

6   Sweeney has trespassed upon me
        and abused me grievously
        and laid violent hands upon me
        to drag me with him from Killarney.

        When Sweeney heard my bell ringing
        he came all of a sudden hurtling
        raving and raging wild against me
        to drive me off and banish me.

        Insult like that – being thrown
        off the ground I'd marked and chosen –
        was too outrageous to endure;
        so God inclined unto my prayer.

        My hand was locked in Sweeney's hand
        until he heard a loud command:
        he was called to Moira, bid to join
        battle with Donal on the plain.

        And so I offered thanks and praise
        for the grace of my release,
        that unpredictable off-chance
        of marching orders from the prince.

        From far off he approached the field

that drove his mind and senses wild.
He shall roam Ireland, mad and bare.
He shall find death on the point of a spear.

The psalter that he grabbed and tore
from me and cast into deep water –
Christ brought it back without a spot.
The psalter stayed immaculate.

A day and a night in brimming waters,
my speckled book was none the worse!
Through the will of God the Son
an otter gave me it again.

This psalter that he profaned
I bequeath with a malediction:
that it bode evil for Colman's race
the day this psalter meets their eyes.

Bare to the world, here came Sweeney
to harass and to harrow me:
therefore, it is God's decree
bare to the world he'll always be.

Eorann, daughter of Conn of Ciannacht,
tried to hold him by his cloak.
Eorann has my blessing for this
but Sweeney lives under my curse.

After that, Ronan came to Moira to make peace   7
between Donal, son of Aodh, and Congal Claon, son
of Scannlan, but he did not succeed. Nevertheless,
the cleric's presence was taken as a seal and guarantee
of the rules of the battle; they made agreements that
no killing would be allowed except between those
hours they had set for beginning and ending the fight
each day. Sweeney, however, would continually violate
every peace and truce which the cleric had ratified,

slaying a man each day before the sides were engaged and slaying another each evening when the combat was finished. Then, on the day fixed for the great battle, Sweeney was in the field before everyone else.

8 He was dressed like this:
   next his white skin, the shimmer of silk;
   and his satin girdle around him;
   and his tunic, that reward of service
   and gift of fealty from Congal,
   was like this –
   crimson, close-woven,
   bordered in gemstones and gold,
   a rustle of sashes and loops,
   the studded silver gleaming,
   the slashed hem embroidered in points.
   He had an iron-shod spear in each hand,
   a shield of mottled horn on his back,
   a gold-hilted sword at his side.

9 He marched out like that until he encountered Ronan with eight psalmists from his community. They were blessing the armies, sprinkling them with holy water, and they sprinkled Sweeney with the rest. Sweeney thought they had done it just to mock him, so he lifted one of his spears, hurled it, and killed one of Ronan's psalmists in a single cast. He made another throw with the second spear at the cleric himself, so that it pierced the bell that hung from his neck, and the shaft sprang off into the air. Ronan burst out:

10 My curse fall on Sweeney
    for his great offence.
    His smooth spear profaned
    my bell's holiness,

    cracked bell hoarding grace
    since the first saint rang it –

it will curse you to the trees,
bird-brain among branches.

Just as the spear-shaft broke
and sprang into the air
may the mad spasms strike
you, Sweeney, forever.

My fosterling lies slain,
your spear-point has been reddened:
to finish off this bargain
you shall die at spear-point.

Should the steadfast tribe of Owen
try to oppose me,
Uradhran and Telle
will visit them with decay.

Uradhran and Telle
have visited them with decay.
Until time dies away
my curse attend you.

My blessing upon Eorann,
that she flourish and grow lovely.
Through everlasting pain
my curse fall on Sweeney.

There were three great shouts as the herded armies   11
clashed and roared out their war cries like stags.
When Sweeney heard these howls and echoes
assumed into the travelling clouds and amplified
through the vaults of space, he looked up and he was
possessed by a dark rending energy.

His brain convulsed,
his mind split open.
Vertigo, hysteria, lurchings

and launchings came over him,
he staggered and flapped desperately,
he was revolted by the thought of known places
and dreamed strange migrations.
His fingers stiffened,
his feet scuffled and flurried,
his heart was startled,
his senses were mesmerized,
his sight was bent,
the weapons fell from his hands
and he levitated in a frantic cumbersome motion
like a bird of the air.
And Ronan's curse was fulfilled.

12 His feet skimmed over the grasses so lightly he
never unsettled a dewdrop and all that day he was
a hurtling visitant of plain and field, bare mountain
and bog, thicket and marshland, and there was no
hill or hollow, no plantation or forest in Ireland that
he did not appear in that day; until he reached Ros
Bearaigh in Glen Arkin, where he hid in a yew tree in
the glen.

13 Donal, son of Aodh, won the battle that day. A
kinsman of Sweeney's called Aongus the Stout
survived and came fleeing with a band of his
people into Glen Arkin. They were wondering
about Sweeney because they had not seen him
alive after the fight and he had not been counted
among the casualties. They were discussing this
and deciding that Ronan's curse had something to
do with it when Sweeney spoke out of the yew:

14   Soldiers, come here.
        You are from Dal-Arie,
        and the man you are looking for
        roosts in his tree.

The life God grants me now
is bare and starved;
I've wasted away, women
shun me, the music has ended.

So I am here at Ros Bearaigh.
Ronan has brought me low,
God has exiled me from myself –
soldiers, forget the man you knew.

When the men heard Sweeney's recitation they knew   15
him at once and tried to persuade him to trust them.
He said he never would, and as they closed round the
tree, he launched himself nimbly and lightly and flew
to Kilreagan in Tyrconnell, where he perched on the
old tree by the church.

It turned out that Donal, son of Aodh, and his
army were there after the battle, and when they saw
the madman lighting in the tree, a crowd of them
ringed and besieged it. They began shouting out
guesses about the creature in the branches; one would
say it was a woman, another that it was a man, until
Donal himself recognized him and said:

– It is Sweeney, the king of Dal-Arie, the man
that Ronan cursed on the day of the battle. That is a
good man up there, he said, and if he wanted wealth
and store he would be welcome to them, if only he
would trust us. I am upset that Congal's people are
reduced to this, for he and I had strong ties before
we faced the battle. But then, Sweeney was warned
by Colmcille when he went over with Congal to ask
the king of Scotland for an army to field against me.
Then Donal uttered the lay:

Sweeney, what has happened here?   16
Sweeney, who led hosts to war
and was the flower among them all
at Moira on that day of battle!

To see you flushed after a feast,
poppy in the gold of harvest!
Hair like shavings or like down,
your natural and perfect crown.

To see your handsome person go
was morning after a fall of snow.
The blue and crystal of your eyes
shone like deepening windswept ice.

Surefooted, elegant, except
you stumbled in the path of kingship,
you were a blooded swordsman, quick
to sense a chance and quick to strike.

Colmcille promised you, good son,
salvation and a royal throne:
how eagerly you strutted forth
blessed by that voice of heaven and earth.

Truthful seer, Colmcille
prophesied in this oracle:
All crossed the sea and here you stand
who'll never all return from Ireland.

Find the answer to his riddle
at Moira on the field of battle,
a gout of blood on a shining blade,
Congal Claon among the dead.

17   When Sweeney heard the shouts of the soldiers
and the big noise of the army, he rose out of the
tree towards the dark clouds and ranged far over
mountains and territories.

A long time he went faring all through Ireland,
poking his way into hard rocky clefts,

shouldering through ivy bushes,
unsettling falls of pebbles in narrow defiles,
wading estuaries,
breasting summits,
trekking through glens,
until he found the pleasures of Glen Bolcain.

That place is a natural asylum where all the madmen of
Ireland used to assemble once their year in madness was
complete.

Glen Bolcain is like this:
it has four gaps to the wind,
pleasant woods, clean-banked wells,
cold springs and clear sandy streams
where green-topped watercress and languid brooklime
philander over the surface.
It is nature's pantry
with its sorrels, its wood-sorrels,
its berries, its wild garlic,
its black sloes and its brown acorns.

The madmen would beat each other for the pick of
its water-cresses and for the beds on its banks.

Sweeney stayed a long time in that glen until one   18
night he was cooped up in the top of a tall ivy-grown
hawthorn. He could hardly endure it, for every time
he twisted or turned, the thorny twigs would flail him
so that he was prickled and cut and bleeding all over.
He changed from that station to another one, a clump
of thick briars with a single young blackthorn standing
up out of the thorny bed, and he settled in the top of
the blackthorn. But it was too slender. It wobbled and
bent so that Sweeney fell heavily through the thicket
and ended up on the ground like a man in a bloodbath.
Then he gathered himself up, exhausted and beaten,
and came out of the thicket, saying:

     – It is hard to bear this life after the pleasant times
I knew. And it has been like this a year to the night
last night!

     Then he spoke this poem:

19   A year until last night
           I have lived among dark trees,
           between the flood and ebb-tide,
           going cold and naked

           with no pillow for my head,
           no human company
           and, so help me, God,
           no spear and no sword.

           No sweet talk with women.
           Instead, I pine
           for cresses, for the clean
           pickings of brooklime.

           No surge of royal blood,
           camped here in solitude;
           no glory flames the wood,
           no friends, no music.

           Tell the truth: a hard lot.
           And no shirking this fate;
           no sleep, no respite,
           no hope for a long time.

           No house, humming full,
           no men, loud with good will,
           nobody to call me king,
           no drink or banqueting.

           A great gulf yawns now
           between me and that retinue,
           between craziness and reason.

Scavenging through the glen

on my mad royal visit:
no pomp or king's circuit
but wild scuttles in the wood.
Heavenly saints! O Holy God!

No skilled musicians' cunning,
no soft discoursing women,
no open-handed giving;
my doom to be a long dying.

Far other than tonight,
far different my plight
the times when with firm hand
I ruled over a good land.

Prospering, smiled upon,
curbing some mighty steed,
I rode high, on the full tide
of good luck and kingship.

That tide has come and gone
and spewed me up in Glen Bolcain,
disabled now, outcast
for the way I sold my Christ,

fallen almost through death's door,
drained out, spiked and torn,
under a hard-twigged bush,
the brown, jaggy hawthorn.

Our sorrows were multiplied
that Tuesday when Congal fell.
Our dead made a great harvest,
our remnant, a last swathe.

This has been my plight.

Fallen from noble heights,
grieving and astray,
a year until last night.

20   He remained in that state in Glen Bolcain until at
last he mustered his strength and flew to Cloonkill
on the borders of Bannagh and Tyrconnell. That
night he went to the edge of the well for a drink of
water and a bite of watercress and after that he went
into the old tree by the church. That was a very bad
night for Sweeney. There was a terrible storm and he
despaired, saying:

   – It is a pity I wasn't killed at Moira instead of
having to put up with hardship like this.

   Then he said this poem:

21   Tonight the snow is cold.
I was at the end of my tether
but hunger and bother
are endless.

Look at me, broken
and down-at-heel,
Sweeney from Rasharkin.
Look at me now

always shifting,
making fresh pads,
and always at night.
At times I am afraid.

In the grip of dread
I would launch and sail
beyond the known seas.
I am the madman of Glen Bolcain,

wind-scourged, stripped
like a winter tree

clad in black frost
and frozen snow.

Hard grey branches
have torn my hands,
the skin of my feet
is in strips from briars

and the pain of frostbite
has put me astray,
from Slemish to Slieve Gullion,
from Slieve Gullion to Cooley.

I went raving with grief
on the top of Croagh Patrick,
from Glen Bolcain to Islay,
from Kintyre to Mourne.

I woke at dawn
with a fasting spittle:
then at Cloonkill, a bunch of cress,
then at Kilnoo, the cuckoo flower.

I wish I lived safe
and sound in Rasharkin
and not here, heartbroken,
in my bare pelt, at bay in the snow.

Sweeney kept going until he reached the church 22
at Swim-Two-Birds on the Shannon, which is now
called Cloonburren; he arrived there on a Friday,
to be exact. The clerics of the church were singing
nones, women were beating flax and one was giving
birth to a child.

— It is unseemly, said Sweeney, for the women to
violate the Lord's fast day. That woman beating the
flax reminds me of our beating at Moira.

Then he heard the vesper bell ringing and said:

– It would be sweeter to listen to the notes of the cuckoos on the banks of the Bann than to the whinge of this bell tonight.

Then he uttered the poem:

23   I perched for rest and imagined
cuckoos calling across water,
the Bann cuckoo, calling sweeter
than church bells that whinge and grind.

Friday is the wrong day, woman,
for you to give birth to a son,
the day when Mad Sweeney fasts
for love of God, in penitence.

Do not just discount me. Listen.
At Moira my tribe was beaten,
beetled, heckled, hammered down,
like flax being scutched by these women.

From the crag of Lough Diolar
up to Derry Colmcille
I saw the great swans, heard their calls
sweetly rebuking wars and battles.

On Solitary cliffs, a stag
bells and makes the whole glen shake
and re-echo. I am ravished.
Unearthly sweetness shakes my breast.

O Christ, the loving and the sinless,
hear my prayer, attend, O Christ,
and let nothing separate us.
Blend me forever in your sweetness.

24   The next day Sweeney went on to St. Derville's church, west of Erris, where he fed on watercress and drank the water that was in the church. The night

was tempestuous, and he was shaken with grief at his misery and deprivation. He was also homesick for Dal-Arie and spoke these verses:

I pined the whole night   25
in Derville's chapel
for Dal-Arie
and peopled the dark

with a thousand ghosts.
My dream restored me:
the army lay at Drumfree
and I came into my kingdom,

camped with my troop,
back with Faolchu and Congal
for our night at Drumduff.
Taunters, will-o'-the-wisps,

who saw me brought to heel
at Moira, you crowd my head
and fade away
and leave me to the night.

Sweeney wandered Ireland for all of the next   26
seven years until one night he arrived back in Glen
Bolcain. That was his ark and his Eden, where he
would go to ground and would only leave when
terror struck. He stayed there that night and the
next morning Lynchseachan arrived looking for
him. Some say Lynchseachan was a half-brother
of Sweeney's, some say he was a foster-brother, but
whichever he was, he was deeply concerned for
Sweeney and brought him back three times out of his
madness.

   This time Lynchseachan was after him in the glen
and found his footprints on the bank of the stream
where Sweeney would go to eat watercress. He

also followed the trail of snapped branches where Sweeney had shifted from tree to tree. But he did not catch up that day, so he went into a deserted house in the glen and lay down, fatigued by all his trailing and scouting. Soon he was in a deep sleep.

Then Sweeney, following the tracks of his tracker, was led to the house and stood listening to the snores of Lynchsea-chan; and consequently he came out with this poem:

27   I dare not sink down, snore and fall
fast asleep like the man at the wall,
I who never batted an eye
during the seven years since Moira.

God of Heaven! Why did I go
battling out that famous Tuesday
to end up changed into Mad Sweeney,
roosting alone up in the ivy?

From the well at Drum Cirb, watercress
supplies my bit and sup at terce;
its juices that have greened my chin
are Sweeney's markings and his birth-stain.

And the manhunt is an expiation.
Mad Sweeney is on the run
and sleeps curled up beneath a rag
under the shadow of Slieve League –

long cut off from the happy time
when I lived apart, an honoured name;
long exiled from those rushy hillsides,
far from my home among the reeds.

I give thanks to the King above
whose harshness only proves His love
which was outraged by my offence

and shaped my new shape for my sins –

shivering; glimpsed against the sky,
a waif alarmed out of the ivy.
Going drenched in teems of rain,
crouching under thunderstorms.

Though I still have life, haunting deep
in the yew glen, climbing mountain slopes,
I would swop places with Congal Claon,
stretched on his back among the slain.

My life is steady lamentation
The roof above my head has gone.
I am doomed to rags, starved and mad,
brought to this by the power of God.

It was sheer madness to imagine
any life outside Glen Bolcain –
Glen Bolcain, my pillow and heart's ease,
my Eden thick with apple trees.

What does he know, the man at the wall,
of Sweeney's trials since his fall?
Going stooped through the long grass.
A sup of water. Watercress.

Summering where herons stalk.
Wintering out among wolf-packs.
Plumed in twigs that green and fall.
What does he know, the man at the wall?

I who once camped among mad friends
in Bolcain, happy glen of winds
and wind-borne echoes, live miserable
beyond the dreams of the man at the wall.

After that poem he arrived, on the following night,   28

at a mill owned by Lynchseachan. The caretaker of
the mill was Lynchseachan's mother-in-law, an old
woman called Lonnog, daughter of Dubh Dithribh.
When Sweeney went in to see her she gave him a few
scraps to eat and so, for a long time, he kept coming
back to the mill.

One day when Lynchseachan was out trailing him,
he caught sight of Sweeney by the mill-stream, and
went to speak to the old woman.

– Has Sweeney come to the mill? said Lynchseachan.

– He was here last night, said the woman.

Lynchseachan then disguised himself as his
mother-in-law and sat on in the mill after she had
gone, until Sweeney arrived that night. But when
Sweeney saw the eyes under the shawl, he recognized
Lynchseachan and at once sprang out of his reach
and up through the skylight, saying:

– This is a pitiful jaunt you are on, Lynchseachan,
hunting me from every place I love in Ireland.
Don't you know Ronan has left me with the fears
of a bird, so I cannot trust you? I am exasperated at
the way you are constantly after me.

And he made this poem:

29   Lynchseachan, you are a bother.
Leave me alone, give me peace.
Is it not enough that Ronan doomed me
to live furtive and suspicious?

When I let fly that fatal spear
at Ronan in the heat of battle
it split his holy breastplate open,
it made a dent in his cleric's bell.

When I nailed him in the battle
with that magnificent spear-cast,
– Let the freedom of the birds be yours!
was how he prayed, Ronan the priest.

And I rebounded off his prayer
up, up and up, flying through air
lighter and nimbler and far higher
than I would ever fly again.

To see me in my morning glory
that Tuesday morning, turn time back:
still in my mind's eye I march out
in rank, in step with my own folk.

But now with my own two eyes I see
a thing that's more astonishing:
under the hood of a woman's shawl,
the weather eyes of Lynchseachan.

– All you intend is to make me ridiculous, he said.   30
Leave off, harass me no more but go back to your
own place and I will go on to see Eorann.

When Sweeney deserted the kingship, his wife   31
had gone to live with Guaire. There had been two
kinsmen with equal rights to the kingship Sweeney
had abandoned, two grandsons of Scannlan's called
Guaire and Eochaidh. At that time, Eorann was with
Guaire and they had gone hunting through the Fews
towards Edenterriff in Cavan. His camp was near
Glen Bolcain, on a plain in the Armagh district.

Sweeney landed on the lintel of Eorann's hut and
spoke to her:

– Do you remember, lady, the great love we shared
when we were together? Life is still a pleasure to you
but not to me.

And this exchange ensued between them:

Sweeney: 32
    Restless as wingbeats
    of memory, I hover

above you, and your bed
still warm from your lover.

Remember when you played
the promise-game with me?
Sun and moon would have died
if ever you lost your Sweeney!

But you have broken trust,
unmade it like a bed –
not mine in the dawn frost
but yours, that he invaded.

Eorann:

Welcome here, my crazy dote,
my first and last and favourite!
I'm easy now, and yet I wasted
at the cruel news of your being bested.

Sweeney:

There's more welcome for the prince
who preens for you and struts
to those amorous banquets
where Sweeney feasted once.

Eorann:

All the same, I would prefer
a hollow tree and Sweeney bare –
that sweetest game we used to play –
to banqueting with him today.

I tell you, Sweeney, if I were given
the pick of all in earth and Ireland,
I'd rather go with you, live sinless
and sup on water and watercress.

Sweeney:

But cold and hard as stone

lies Sweeney's path
through the beds of Lisardowlin.
There I go to earth

in panic, starved and bare,
a rickle of skin and bones.
I am yours no longer.
And you are another man's.

Eorann:

My poor tormented lunatic!
When I see you like this it makes me sick
your cheek gone pale, your skin all scars,
ripped and scored by thorns and briars.

Sweeney:

And yet I hold no grudge,
my gentle one.
Christ ordained my bondage
and exhaustion.

Eorann:

I wish we could fly away together,
be rolling stones, birds of a feather:
I'd swoop to pleasure you in flight
and huddle close on the roost at night.

Sweeney:

I have gone north and south.
One night I was in the Mournes.
I have wandered as far as the Bann mouth
and Kilsooney.

They had no sooner finished than the army swept
into the camp from every side, and as usual, he was
away in a panic, never stopping until twilight, when
he arrived at Ros Bearaigh – that church where he
first halted after the battle of Moira – and again

33

he went into the yew tree of the church. Murtagh McEarca was erenach of the church at the time and his wife was passing the yew when by chance she caught sight of the madman. Recognizing Sweeney, she said:

– Come down out of the yew. I know you are king of Dal-Arie, and there is nobody here but myself, a woman on her own.

That is what she said, though she hoped to beguile him somehow into a trap and catch him.

– Indeed I shall not come down, said Sweeney, for Lynchseachan and his wife might come upon me. But am I not hard to recognize nowadays?

And he uttered these stanzas:

34   Only your hawk eye
could pick me out
who was cock of the walk once
in Dal-Arie –

the talk of Ireland
for style and appearance.
Since the shock of battle
I'm a ghost of myself.

So, good woman, mind
your husband and your house.
I cannot stay. We shall meet
again on Judgement Day.

35   He cleared the tree lightly and nimbly and went on his way until he reached the old tree in Rasharkin, which was one of the three hide-outs he had in his own country, the others being at Teach mic Ninnedha and Cluan Creamha. He lodged undiscovered there for six weeks in the yew tree but he was detected in the end and the nobles of Dal-Arie held a meeting to decide who should go to apprehend him.

Lynchseachan was the unanimous choice and he agreed to go.

Off he went to the tree and there was Sweeney, perched on a branch above him.

– It is a pity, Sweeney, he said, that you ended up like this, like any bird of the air, without food or drink or clothes, you that went in silk and satin and rode foreign steeds in their matchless harness. Do you remember your train, the lovely gentle women, the many young men and their hounds, the retinue of craftsmen? Do you remember the assemblies under your sway? Do you remember the cups and goblets and carved horns that flowed with pleasant heady drink? It is a pity to find you like any poor bird flitting from one waste ground to the next.

– Stop now, said Sweeney, it was my destiny. But have you any news for me about my country?

– I have indeed, said Lynchseachan, for your father is dead.

– That is a seizure, he said.

– Your mother is dead too, said the young man.

– There'll be pity from nobody now, he said.

– And your brother, said Lynchseachan.

– My side bleeds for that, said Sweeney.

– Your daughter is dead, said Lynchseachan.

– The heart's needle is an only daughter, said Sweeney.

– And your son who used to call you Daddy, said Lynchseachan.

– Indeed, he said, that is the drop that fells me to the ground.

After that, Sweeney and Lynchseachan made up this poem between them:

Lynchseachan: 36
  Sweeney from the high mountains,
  blooded swordsman, veteran:
  for the sake of Christ, your judge and saviour,

speak to me, your foster-brother.

If you hear me, listen. Listen,
my royal lord, my great prince,
for I bring, as gently as I can,
the bad news from your home ground.

You left behind a dead kingdom
and that is why I had to come
with tidings of a dead brother,
a father dead, a dead mother.

Sweeney:
If my gentle mother's dead, I face
a harder exile from my place;
yet she had cooled in love of me
and love that's cooled is worse than pity.

The son whose father's lately dead
kicks the trace and lives unbridled.
His pain's a branch bowed down with nuts.
A dead brother is a wounded side.

Lynchseachan:
Things that the world already knows
I still must break to you as news:
thin as you are, and starved, your wife
pined after you, and died of grief.

Sweeney:
A household when the wife is gone,
a boat that's rudderless in storm;
it is pens of feathers next the skin;
a widower at his bleak kindling.

Lynchseachan:
Sorrow accumulates: heartbreak,
keens and wailings fill the air.

But all of that's like a fist round smoke
now that you have lost your sister.

Sweeney:

No common wisdom I might invoke
can stanch the wound from such a stroke.
A sister's love is still, unselfish,
like sunlight mild upon a ditch.

Lynchseachan:

Our north is colder than it was,
calves are kept in from their cows
since your daughter and sister's son,
who both loved you, were stricken down.

Sweeney:

My faithful hound, my faithful nephew –
no bribe could buy their love of me.
But you've unstitched the rent of sorrow.
The heart's needle is an only daughter.

Lynchseachan:

I tell now what I would keep back.
It wounds me to the very quick!
In Dal-Arie, everyone
laments the death of your son.

Sweeney:

This is the news that daunts all men.
This is the thing that brings us down –
the loss, the wound in memory,
the death of him who called me *Daddy*.

This is a blow I cannot stand.
Here resistance has to end
You are the beater, I the bird
scared and driven out of covert.

Lynchseachan:
>   Sweeney, now you are in my hands,
>   I tell you I can heal these wounds.
>   None of your family's in the grave.
>   All your people are alive.
>
>   Calm yourself. Come to. Rest.
>   Come home east. Forget the west.
>   Admit, Sweeney, you have come too far
>   from where your heart's affections are.
>
>   Woods and forests and wild deer –
>   things like these delight you more
>   than sleeping in your eastern dun
>   on a bed of feather-down.
>
>   Near a quick mill-pond, your perch
>   on a dark green holly branch
>   means more now than any feast
>   among the brightest and the best.
>
>   Harp music in the breasting hills
>   would not soothe you: you would still
>   strain to hear from the oak-wood
>   the brown stag belling to the herd.
>
>   Swifter than the wind in glens,
>   once the figure of a champion,
>   now a legend, and a madman –
>   your exile's over, Sweeney. Come.

37   When Sweeney heard the news of his only son he
fell from the yew tree and Lynchseachan caught him
and put manacles on him. Then he told him that all
his people were alive, and escorted him back to the
assembled nobles of Dal-Arie. They produced locks
and fetters in which they shackled Sweeney and left

him under Lynchseachan's supervision for the next six weeks. During that time the nobles of the province kept visiting him, and at the end of it, his sense and memory came back to him and he felt himself restored to his old shape and manner. So they took the tackle off him and he was back to his former self, the man they had known as king.

After that, Sweeney was quartered in Lynchseachan's bedroom. Then harvest time came round and one day Lynchseachan went with his people to reap. Sweeney, shut in the bedroom, was left in the care of the mill-hag, who was warned not to speak to him. All the same, she did speak to him, asking him to relate some of his adventures when he was in his state of madness.

– A curse on your mouth, hag, said Sweeney, for your talk is dangerous. God will not allow me to go mad again.

– It was your insult to Ronan that put you mad, said the hag.

– This is hateful, he said, to have to put up with your treachery and trickery.

– It is no treachery, only the truth.

And Sweeney said:

Sweeney: 38
> Hag, did you come here from your mill
> to spring me over wood and hill?
> Is it to be a woman's ploy
> and treachery send me astray?

The Hag:
> Sweeney, your sorrows are well known,
> and I am not the treacherous one:
> the miracles of holy Ronan
> maddened and drove you among madmen.

Sweeney:
> If I were king and I wish I were

again the king who held sway here,
instead of the banquet and ale-mug
I'd give you a fist on the mouth, hag.

39   – Now listen, woman, he said, if you only knew the
hard times I have been through. Many's the dreadful
leap I have leaped from hill and fort and land and
valley.
    – For God's sake, said the hag, let me see one of
those leaps now. Show me how you did it when you
were off in your madness.
    With that, he bounded over the bed-rail and lit on
the end of the bench.
    – Sure I could do that leap myself, said the hag,
and she did it.
    Then Sweeney took another leap out through the
skylight of the lodge.
    – I could do that too, said the hag, and leaped it,
there and then.
    Anyhow, this is the way it ended up: Sweeney
went lifting over five cantreds of Dal-Arie that
day until he arrived at Gleann na n-Eachtach in
Feegile and she was on his heels the whole way.
When he took a rest there, in the top of an ivy-
bunch, the hag perched on another tree beside him.
    It was the end of the harvest season and Sweeney
heard a hunting-call from a company in the skirts of
the wood.
    – This will be the outcry of the Ui Faolain coming
to kill me, he said. I slew their king at Moira and this
host is out to avenge him.
    He heard the stag bellowing and he made a poem
in which he praised aloud all the trees of Ireland, and
rehearsed some of his own hardships and sorrows,
saying:

40   Suddenly this bleating
       and belling in the glen!

The little timorous stag
like a scared musician

startles my heartstrings
with high homesick refrains –
deer on my lost mountains,
flocks out on the plain.

The bushy leafy oak tree
is highest in the wood,
the forking shoots of hazel
hide sweet hazel-nuts.

The alder is my darling,
all thornless in the gap,
some milk of human kindness
coursing in its sap.

The blackthorn is a jaggy creel
stippled with dark sloes;
green watercress in thatch on wells
where the drinking blackbird goes.

Sweetest of the leafy stalks,
the vetches strew the pathway;
the oyster-grass is my delight
and the wild strawberry.

Low-set clumps of apple trees
drum down fruit when shaken;
scarlet berries clot like blood
on mountain rowan.

Briars curl in sideways,
arch a stickle back,
draw blood and curl up innocent
to sneak the next attack.

The yew tree in each churchyard
wraps night in its dark hood.
Ivy is a shadowy
genius of the wood.

Holly rears its windbreak,
a door in winter's face;
life-blood on a spear-shaft
darkens the grain of ash.

Birch tree, smooth and blessed,
delicious to the breeze,
high twigs plait and crown it
the queen of trees.

The aspen pales
and whispers, hesitates:
a thousand frightened scuts
race in its leaves.

But what disturbs me most
in the leafy wood
is the to and fro and to and fro
of an oak rod.

Ronan was dishonoured,
he rang his cleric's bell:
my spasm and outrage
brought curse and miracle.

And noble Congal's armour,
his tunic edged in gold,
swathed me in doomed glory
with omens in each fold.

His lovely tunic marked me
in the middle of the rout,
the host pursuing, shouting:

– The one in the gold coat!

Get him, take him live or dead,
every man fall to.
Draw and quarter, pike
and spit him, none will blame you.

Still the horsemen followed
across the north of Down,
my back escaping nimbly
from every javelin thrown.

As if I had been cast
by a spearsman, I flew high,
my course a whisper in the air,
a breeze flicking through ivy.

I overtook the startled fawn,
kept step with his fleet step,
I caught, I rode him lightly –
from peak to peak we leapt,

mountain after mountain,
a high demented spree
from Inishowen south,
and south, as far as Galtee.

From Galtee to Liffey
I was swept along and driven
through bitter twilight
to the slopes of Benn Bulben.

And that was the first night
of my long restless vigil:
my last night at rest,
the eve of Congal's battle.

And then Glen Bolcain was my lair,

my earth and den;
I've scaled and strained against those slopes
by star and moon.

I wouldn't swop a lonely hut
in that dear glen
for a world of moorland
on a russet mountain.

Its water flashing like wet grass,
its wind so keen,
its tall brooklime, its watercress
the greenest green.

I love the ancient ivy tree,
the pale-leafed sallow,
the birth's sibilant melody,
the solemn yew.

And you, Lynchseachan, can try
disguise, deceit;
come in the mask and shawl of night,
I won't be caught.

You managed it the first time
with your litany of the dead:
father, mother, daughter, son,
brother, wife – you lied

but if you want your say again,
then be ready
to face the heights and crags of Mourne
to follow me.

I would live happy
in an ivy bush
high in some twisted tree
and never come out.

The skylarks rising
into their high space
send me pitching and tripping
over stumps on the moor

and my hurry flushes
the turtle dove.
I overtake it,
my plumage rushing,

am startled then
by the startled woodcock
or a blackbird's sudden
volubility.

Think of my alarms,
my coming to earth
where the fox still
gnaws at the bones,

my wild career
as the wolf from the wood
goes tearing ahead
and I rise towards the mountain,

the bark of foxes
echoing below me,
the wolves behind me
howling and rending –

their vapoury tongues,
their low-slung speed
shaken off like nightmare
at the foot of the slope.

If I show my heels
I am hobbled by guilt.

I am a sheep
without a fold

who sleeps his sound sleep
in the old tree at Kilnoo,
dreaming back the good days
with Congal in Antrim.

A starry frost will come
dropping on the pools
and I'll be out
on unsheltered hills:

herons calling
in cold Glenelly,
flocks of birds quickly
coming and going.

I prefer the scurry
and song of blackbirds
to the usual blather
of men and women.

I prefer the squeal
of badgers in their sett
to the hullabuloo
of the morning hunt.

I prefer the re-
echoing belling of a stag
among the peaks
to that terrible horn.

Those unharnessed runners
from glen to glen!
Nobody tames
that royal blood,

each one aloof
on its rightful summit,
antlered, watchful.
Imagine them,

the stag of high Slieve Felim,
the stag of the steep Fews,
the stag of Duhallow, the stag of Orrery,
the fierce stag of Killarney.

The stag of Islandmagee, Larne's stag,
the stag of Moylinny,
the stag of Cooley, the stag of Cunghill,
the stag of the two-peaked Burren.

The mother of this herd
is old and grey,
the stags that follow her
are branchy, many-tined.

I would be cloaked in the grey
covert of her head,
I would roost among
her mazy antlers

and would be lofted into
this thicket of horns
on the stag that lows at me
over the glen.

I am Sweeney, the whinger,
the scuttler in the valley.
But call me, instead,
Peak-pate, Stag-head.

The springs I always liked
were the one at Dunmall
and the well on Knocklayde

that tasted pure and cool.

Mendicant forever,
frayed, scant and raggedy,
high in the mountains
like a crazed, frost-bitten sentry

I find no bed, no quarter,
no place in the sun –
not even in this reddening
covert of tall fern.

My only rest: eternal
sleep in holy ground
when Moling's earth lets fall
dark balm on my wound.

But now that sudden bleating
and belling in the glen!
I am a timorous stag
feathered by Ronan Finn.

41 After that poem, Sweeney went on from Feegile
through Bannagh, Benevenagh and Maghera but
he could not shake off the hag until he reached
Dunseverick in Ulster. There he leaped from the
summit of the fort, down a sheer drop, coaxing
the hag to follow. She leaped quickly after him
but fell on the cliff of Dunseverick, where she was
smashed to pieces and scattered into the sea. That
is how she got her end on Sweeney's trail.

42 Then Sweeney said:
    – From now on, I won't tarry in Dal-Arie because
Lynchseachan would have my life to avenge the hag's.
    So he proceeded to Roscommon in Connacht,
where he alighted on the bank of the well and treated
himself to watercress and water. But when a woman

came out of the erenach's house, he panicked and
fled, and she gathered the watercress from the stream.
Sweeney watched her from his tree and greatly
lamented the theft of his patch of cress, saying:

 – It is a shame that you are taking my watercress.
If only you knew my plight, how I am unpitied by
tribesman or kinsman, how I am no longer a guest in
any house on the ridge of the world. Watercress is my
wealth, water is my wine, and hard bare trees and soft
tree bowers are my friends. Even if you left that cress,
you would not be left wanting; but if you take it, you
are taking the bite from my mouth.

   And he made this poem:

Woman, picking the watercress   43
and scooping up my drink of water,
were you to leave them as my due
you would still be none the poorer.

Woman, have consideration!
We two go two different ways:
I perch out among tree-tops,
you lodge here in a friendly house.

Woman, have consideration.
Think of me in the sharp wind,
forgotten, past consideration,
without a cloak to wrap me in.

Woman, you cannot start to know
sorrows Sweeney has forgotten:
how friends were so long denied him
he killed his gift for friendship even.

Fugitive, deserted, mocked
by memories of my days as king,
no longer called to head the troop
when warriors are mustering,

no longer the honoured guest
at tables anywhere in Ireland,
ranging like a mad pilgrim
over rock-peaks on the mountain.

The harper who harped me to rest,
where is his soothing music now?
My people too, my kith and kin,
where did their affection go?

In my heyday, on horseback,
I rode high into my own:
now memory's an unbroken horse
that rears and suddenly throws me down.

Over starlit moors and plains,
woman plucking my watercress,
to his cold and lonely station
the shadow of that Sweeney goes

with watercress for his herds
and cold water for his mead,
bushes for companions,
the naked hillside for his bed.

Hugging these, my cold comforts,
ever hungering after cress,
above the bare plain of Emly
I hear cries of the wild geese,

and still bowed to my hard yoke,
still a bag of skin and bone,
I reel as if a blow hit me
and fly off at the cry of a heron

to land in Dairbre, maybe,
in spring, when days are on the turn,

to scare away again by twilight
westward, into the Mournes.

Gazing down at clean gravel,
to lean out over a cool well,
drink a mouthful of sunlit water
and gather cress by the handful –

even this you would pluck from me,
lean pickings that have thinned my blood
and chilled me on the cold uplands,
hunkering low when winds spring up.

Morning wind is the coldest wind,
it flays me of my rags, it freezes –
the very memory leaves me speechless,
woman, picking the watercress.

Woman:

Sweeney, be merciful to me.
Leave retribution to the Lord.
Judge not and you won't be judged
Triumph and bless. Do not be hard.

Sweeney:

Then here is justice, fair and even,
from my high court in the yew:
if you leave the cress for me,
I shall leave my rags in lieu.

I have no place to lay my head.
Human love has failed me. So
let me swop sins for cress,
let me make a scapegoat of you.

Your greed has left me hungering.
Therefore, may all you robbed me of
come between you and good luck

and leave you hungering for love.

As you snatched cress, may you be snatched
by the foraging, blue-coated Norse.
And live eaten by remorse.
And cursing God that our paths crossed.

44   He stayed in Roscommon that night and the next
day he went on to Slieve Aughty, from there to the
pleasant slopes of Slemish, then on to the high peaks
of Slieve Bloom, and from there to Inishmurray. After
that, he stayed six weeks in a cave that belonged to
Donnan on the island of Eig off the west of Scotland.
From there he went on to Ailsa Craig, where he spent
another six weeks, and when he finally left there he
bade the place farewell and bewailed his state, like
this:

45   Without bed or board
I face dark days
in frozen lairs
and wind-driven snow.

Ice scoured by winds.
Watery shadows from weak sun.
Shelter from the one tree
on a plateau.

Haunting deerpaths,
enduring rain,
first-footing the grey
frosted grass.

I climb towards the pass
and the stag's belling
rings off the wood,
surf-noise rises

where I go, heartbroken
and worn out,
sharp-haunched Sweeney,
raving and moaning.

The sough of the winter night,
my feet packing the hailstones
as I pad the dappled
banks of Mourne

or lie, unslept, in a wet bed
on the hills by Lough Erne,
tensed for first light
and an early start.

Skimming the waves
at Dunseverick,
listening to billows
at Dun Rodairce,

hurtling from that great wave
to the wave running
in tidal Barrow,
one night in hard Dun Cernan,

the next among the wild flowers
of Benn Boirne;
and then a stone pillow
on the screes of Croagh Patrick.

I shift restlessly
on the plain of Boroma,
from Benn Iughoine
to Benn Boghaine.

Then that woman
interfered,
disturbed me

and affronted me

and made off with
the bite from my mouth.
It is retribution
and it is constant.

I gather cress
in delicious bunches,
four round handfuls
in Glen Bolcain,

and then I unpick
the shy bog-berry,
then drink water
from Ronan's well.

My nails are bent,
my loins weak,
my feet bleeding,
my thighs bare –

and I'll be overtaken
by a stubborn band
of Ulstermen
faring through Scotland.

But to have ended up
lamenting here
on Ailsa Craig.
A hard station!

Ailsa Craig,
the seagulls' home,
God knows it is
hard lodgings.

Ailsa Craig,

bell-shaped rock,
reaching sky-high,
snout in the sea –

it hard-beaked,
me seasoned and scraggy:
we mated like a couple
of hard-shanked cranes.

I tread the slop
and foam of beds,
unlooked for,
penitential,

and imagine treelines
far away,
a banked-up, soothing,
wooded haze,

not like the swung
depths and swells
of that nightmare-black
lough in Mourne.

I need woods
for consolation,
some grove in Meath –
or the space of Ossory.

Or Ulster in harvest.
Strangford, shimmering.
Or a summer visit
to green Tyrone.

At Lammas I migrate
to the pools of Teltown,
pass the springtime fishing
bends of the Shannon.

I often get as far
as my old domain,
those groomed armies,
those stern hillsides.

46   Then Sweeney left Ailsa Craig and flew over the
stormy mass of the sea to the land of the Britons.
He passed their royal stronghold on his right and
discovered a great wood where he could hear wailing
and lamentation. Sometimes it was a great moan of
anguish, sometimes an exhausted sigh. The moaner
turned out to be another madman astray in the wood.
Sweeney approached him.

 – Who are you, friend? Sweeney asked.

 – A madman, said he.

 – In that case, you are a friend indeed. I am a
madman myself, said Sweeney. Why don't you join up
with me?

 – I would, the other man said, except that I am in
dread of the king or the king's retinue capturing me,
and I am not sure that you are not one of them.

 – I am no such thing, said Sweeney, and since you
can trust me, tell me your name.

 – They call me the Man of the Wood, said the madman.

Then Sweeney spoke this verse and the Man of the
Wood answered as follows:

47   *Sweeney:*
What happened, Man of the Wood,
to make you whinge
and hobble like this? Why did
your mind unhinge?

Man:
Caution and fear of the king
have silenced me.

I made a tombstone of my tongue
to keep my story.

I am the Man of the Wood.
I was famous
in battles once. Now I hide
among bushes.

Sweeney:
I come from the Bush myself.
I am Sweeney,
son of Colman. Like yourself,
outcast, shifty.

After that, they did confide in each other and shared 48
their life stories. Sweeney said to the madman:
  – Tell me about yourself.
  – I am a landowner's son, said the mad Briton, a
native of this country, and my name is Alan.
  – Tell me, Sweeney asked, what made you mad?
  – It is simple. Once upon a time there were two
kings in this country, struggling for the kingship. Their
names were Eochaidh and Cuagu. Eochaidh was the
better king and I am one of his people. Anyhow, the
issue was to be decided at a great muster where there
was to be a battle. I laid solemn obligations on each
of my chief's people that none was to come to the
battle unless he was arrayed in silk. I did this so that
they would be magnificent, outstanding beyond the
others in pomp and panoply. But, for doing that, the
hosts cursed me with three howls of malediction that
sent me astray and frightened, the way you see me.

In the same way he asked Sweeney what drove him to 49
madness.
  – The words of Ronan, said Sweeney. At the battle
of Moira he cursed me in front of the armies so that
I sprang out of the battle and have been wandering

and fleeing ever since.

    – O Sweeney, said Alan, since we have trusted each other, let us now be guardians to each other.

> Whoever of us is the first to hear
> the cry of a heron from a lough's blue-green waters
> or the clear note of a cormorant
> or the flight of a woodcock off a branch
> or the wheep of a plover disturbed in its sleep
> or the crackle of feet in withered branches,
> or whoever of us is the first to see
> the shadow of a bird above the wood,
> let him warn the other.
> Let us move always
> with the breadth of two trees between us.
> And if one of us hears any of these things
> or anything like them,
> let both of us scatter immediately.

50   So they went about like that for a year. At the end of the year Alan said to Sweeney:

    – Today is the day we must part, for the end of my life has come, and I will go where I am destined to meet my death.

    – How will you die? Sweeney asked.

    – That is simple, Alan said. I will proceed now to the waterfall at Doovey, where a blast of wind will unbalance me and pitch me into the waterfall, so that I'll be drowned. Afterwards, I will be buried in the churchyard of a saint. And I'll go to heaven. And now, Sweeney, said Alan, tell me what your own fate will be.

    Sweeney told him what this story goes on to tell and they parted. The Briton set out for the waterfall and when he reached it he was drowned in it.

51   Then Sweeney came to Ireland, reaching the plain of Moylinny, in Antrim, as the evening was drawing on.

When he realized where he was, he said:

– This was always a good plain, and I was here once with a good man. That was Scannlan's son, my friend Congal Claon. One day here I said to Congal that I wanted to go to another lord and master because the rewards I got from him were too small. To persuade me to stay with him, Congal immediately gave me a hundred and fifty lovely horses, and his own brown steed into the bargain; and a hundred and fifty flashing swords, hafted in tusks; fifty servants and fifty servant girls; a tunic made of cloth-of-gold, and a magnificent girdle of chequered silk.

Then Sweeney recited this poem:

Now my bare skin feels
night falling on Moylinny,
the plain where Congal lived.
Now in my memory

I see Congal and me
riding across the plain
deep in conversation,
headed for Drum Lurgan.

I am saying to the king:
– The services I give
are not being rewarded.
And I threaten I will leave.

What does the king do then?
He gives me in their hundreds
horses, bridles, swords, foreign
captives, girl attendants.

And my great chestnut steed,
the best that grazed or galloped,
his cloth-of-gold tunic,
his girdle of silk plaits.

So what plain matches this plain?
Is it the plain of Meath
or the plain of Airgeadros
or Moyfevin with its crosses?

Moylurg or Moyfea,
the lovely plain of Connacht,
the Liffey banks, Bannside,
or the plain of Muirhevna?

I have seen all of them,
north, south, east, and west,
but never saw the equal
of this ground in Antrim.

53   When he had made that poem Sweeney came on to
Glen Bolcain, where he went wandering freely until
he met with a madwoman. He shied and ran away
from her, yet divining somehow that she too was
simple-minded, he stopped in his tracks and turned to
her. With that, she shied and ran away from him.
     – Alas, God, Sweeney said, life is a misery. I scare
away from her and she scares away from me. And in
Glen Bolcain, of all places!
     Then he began:

54   Whoever stirs up enmity
should never have been born;
may every bitter man and woman
be barred at the gate of heaven.

If three conspire and combine
one will backbite or complain
as I complain, going torn
by briar and sharp blackthorn.

First, madwoman flees from man.

Then, it's something stranger even:
barefoot, in his bare skin,
The man is running from the woman.

In November, wild ducks fly.
From those dark evenings until May
let us forage, nest and hide
in ivy in the brown-floored wood

and hear behind the late birds' song
sounds of water in Glen Bolcain,
its streams that hurry, hush and jabber,
its islands in the forking rivers,

its hazel trees, holly bowers,
its leaves, its acorns, its briars,
its nuts, its sharp-tasting sloes,
its cool-fleshed winter-berries:

and under trees, its hounds coursing,
its dappled antlered stags belling,
its waters' endless, endless fall –
sounds of water in Glen Bolcain.

After that, Sweeney went to the house where his 55
wife, Eorann, was lodging with her retinue of maid-
servants. He stood at the outer door of the house and
spoke to his former queen:

– Here you are, Eorann, laid in the lap of luxury,
and still there is no lap for me to lie in.

– That is how it is, Eorann said, but come in.

– Indeed I will not, said Sweeney, in case the army
traps me in the house.

– Well, said the woman, it seems your mind has
not got any better, and since you don't want to stop
with us, why don't you go away and leave us in peace?
There are people here who knew you when you were
in your right mind; it would be an embarrassment if

they were to see you like this.

– Isn't that terrible, said Sweeney. Now I know it. It is fatal to trust a woman. And I was generous to this one. She is spurning me now but I would have been the man of the moment if I had come back that day when I slew Oilill Caedach, the king of Ui Faolain.

And with that he said:

56
Any man a woman falls for,
however handsome, should beware.
Sweeney is the living proof,
he was cast off by his love.

Any trusting man must stay
on guard against their treachery:
betrayal such as mine by Eorann
is second nature in a woman.

Gullible, open-handed,
straightforward, wide-eyed,
I gave my steeds and herds away,
filled her pastures in a day.

In the thick of fighting men
I could more than hold my own:
when the battle cry was sounded
I handled thirty single-handed.

It was Congal's right to ask for
a warrior to champion Ulster:
– Who among you will take on
the fighter king of Ui Faolain?

Oilill was a berserk giant,
a shield and spear in either hand,
so overbearing in his stride
for a while our ranks were daunted.

But when I spoke at Congal's side
I didn't whinge, I didn't backslide:
– Though Oilill be their strongest bastion,
I will hold the line against him.

I left him shortened by a head
and left the torso, and exulted,
and left five other princes dead
before I stopped to wipe my blade.

With that, Sweeney rose lightly and stealthily and 57
went hopping airily from peak to peak, from one hill
to the next, until he reached Mourne in the south of
Ulster. He rested there, saying:
– This is a good place for a madman, but it is
no place for corn or milk or food. And though it is
a lovely, lofty station, it is still uncomfortable and
uneasy. There is no shelter here from the storm or the
shower.
And then he uttered these words:

The Mournes are cold tonight, 58
my quarters are desolate:
no milk or honey in this land
of snowdrift and gusting wind.

In a sharp-branched holly tree
I shiver and waste away,
chilled to the bone, camped out
up here on the naked summit.

The pools are ice, frost hardens on me.
Then I shake and break free,
coming alive like a fanned ember
in winds sweeping north from Leinster,

dreaming dreams of autumn days
round Hallowe'en and All Hallows,

longing for my old ground –
the clear waters of Glen Bolcain.

Astray no more then east or west,
blizzards whipping my bare face,
atremble no more in some den,
a starved, pinched, raving madman,

but sheltered in that drappled arbour,
my haven, my winter harbour,
my refuge from the bare heath,
my royal fort, my king's rath.

Every night I glean and raid
and comb the floor of the oak wood.
My hands work into leaf and rind,
roots, windfalls on the ground,

they rake through matted watercress
and grope among the bog-berries,
cool brooklime, sorrel, damp moss,
wild garlic and raspberries,

apples, hazel-nuts, acorns,
the haws of sharp, jaggy hawthorns,
blackberries, the floating weed,
the whole store of the oak wood.

Keep me here, Christ, far away
from open ground and flat country.
Let me suffer the cold of glens.
I dread the cold of open plains.

59   The next morning Sweeney started again. He passed
Moyfevin and the clear, green-wavering Shannon; he
passed the inviting slopes of Aughty, the spreading
pastures of Loughrea, the delightful banks of the
River Suck, and landed on the shores of broad

Lough Ree. He spent that night in the fork of Bile Tiobradain, which was one of his favourite hideouts in the country. It was in Creegaille, in the east of Connacht.

Great sorrow and misery descended on him and he said:

– Indeed I have suffered trouble and distress. It was cold in the Mournes last night and it is no better tonight in the fork of Bile Tiobradain.

It was snowing that night, and as fast as the snow fell, it was frozen. So he said: 60

– I have endured purgatories since the feathers grew on me. And still there is no respite. I realize, he said, that even if it were to mean my death, it would be better to trust my people than to endure these woes forever.

Then he recited the poem, proclaiming aloud his woes:

Almighty God, I deserved this, 61
my cut feet, my drained face,
winnowed by a sheer wind
and miserable in my mind.

Last night I lay in Mourne
plastered in wet; cold rain poured.
Tonight, in torment, in Glasgally
I am crucified in the fork of a tree.

I who endured unflinchingly
through long nights and long days
since the feathers penned my frame
foresee nothing but the same.

Hard weather has withered me,
blizzards have buried me.
As I wince here in cutting wind

Glen Bolcain's heather haunts my mind.

Unsettled, panicky, astray,
I course over the whole country
from River Liffey to Lower Bann,
from Bannside to the banks of Lagan;

then over Rathmore to Roscommon,
and fields that lie around Cruachan,
above Moylurg's level plain
and the brow of bushy Fews Mountain.

Or else I make a tough migration
to the Knockmealdown mountains;
or from Glasgally, a long glide
eastward to a Louth hillside.

All this is hard to thole, Lord!
Still without bed or board,
crouching to graze on cress,
drinking cold water from rivers.

Alarmed out of the autumn wood,
whipped by whins, flecked with blood,
running wild among wolf-packs,
shying away with the red stag.

Son of God, have mercy on us!
Never to hear a human voice!
To sleep naked every night
up there in the highest thickets,

to have lost my proper shape and looks,
a mad scuttler on mountain peaks,
a derelict doomed to loneliness:
Son of God, have mercy on us!

62   – All the same, Sweeney said, even if Donal, son of

Aodh, were to kill me, I should still go to Dal-Arie and trust to the mercy of my own people. If the mill-hag had not duped me into that bout of leaping, I would still be sane enough.

Then a glimmer of reason came back to him and he set out for his own country, ready to settle there and entrust himself to the people. 63

Ronan heard of Sweeney's return to his senses and his decision to go back among his own, and cried out:

– I beseech you, Lord, that the persecutor come not near the church to torment it again; I beseech you, do not relent in your vengeance or ease his affliction until he is sundered body from soul in his death-swoon. Remember that you struck him for an example, a warning to tyrants that you and your people were sacred and not to be lightly dishonoured or outraged.

God answered Ronan's prayer. When Sweeney was out on the uplands of the Fews he halted, stalk still: a strange apparition rose before him at midnight. Bleeding headless torsos and disembodied heads – five scraggy, goat-bearded heads – screamed and bounced this way and that over the road. When he got among them, they were talking to each other. 64

– He is a madman, said the first head.
– A madman from Ulster, said the second.
– Follow him well, said the third.
– May the pursuit be long, said the fourth.
– Until he reaches the sea, said the fifth.

They rose in a flock, coming for him, but he soared away in front, skimming from thicket to thicket; and no matter how wide the glen that opened before him, he bounded from edge to edge, from the top of one hill to the top of the next.

The heads were pursuing him, 65

lolling and baying,
snapping and yelping,
whining and squealing.

They nosed at his calves and his thighs,
they breathed on his shoulder,
they nuzzled the back of his neck,
they went bumping off tree-trunks and rock-face,
they spouted and plunged like a waterfall,
until he gave them the slip and escaped
in a swirling tongue of low cloud.

66   He had lost them, goat-head and dog-head and
the whole terrifying pack he had sensed there. But
his previous wandering and flying were nothing
compared with what he suffered now, for he was
startled into a fit which lasted six weeks until he
perched one night in the top of a tree, on the summit
of Slieve Eidhneach. In the morning he began
lamenting:

67   My dark night has come round again.
The world goes on but I return
to haunt myself. I freeze and burn.
I am the bare figure of pain.

Frost crystals and the level ice,
the scourging snow, the male-voiced storm
they all perform my requiem.
My hearth goes cold, my fire dies.

Are there still some who call me prince?
The King of Kings, the Lord of All
revoked my title, worked my downfall,
unhoused, unwived me for my sins.

Why did He spare my life at Moira?
Why did He grudge me death in battle?

Why ordained the hag of the mill
His hound of heaven and my fury?

The mill-hag's millstone round my neck!
Hell roast her soul! She dragged me down
when I leaped up in agitation.
I fell for that old witch's trick.

Then Lynchseachan was in full cry,
a bloodhound never off my trail.
I fell for his lies too and fell
among captors out of the tree.

They made me face the love I'd lost.
They tied me up and carried me
back to the house. The mockery!
I overheard their victory feast

yet gradually grew self-possessed,
for there were kindly people there,
and gaming and constant laughter.
My mind was knitting up at last

but soon unravelled into nightmare.
I was for the high jump once more.
The mill-hag spun her web and swore
her innocence. I leaped for her

and leaped beyond the bounds of sense.
She challenged me a second time.
We kept in step like words in rhyme.
I set the pace and led the dance –

I cleared the skylight and the roof,
I flew away beyond the fortress
but she hung on. Through smooth and rough
I raised the wind and led the chase.

We coursed all over Ireland then.
I was the wind and she was smoke.
I was the prow and she the wake.
I was the earth and she the moon.

But always look before you leap!
Though she was fit for bog and hill,
Dunseverick gave her the spill.
She followed me down off the top

of the fort and spread-eagled
her bitch's body in the air.
I trod the water, watching her
hit the rocks. And I was glad

to see her float in smithereens.
A crew of devils made a corpse
of her and buried it. Oh, cursed
be the ground that housed her bones!

One night I walked across the Fews –
the hills were dark, the starlight dead –
when suddenly five severed heads,
five lantern ghouls, appeared and rose

like bats from hell, surrounding me.
Then a head spoke – another shock!
– This is the Ulster lunatic.
Let us drive him into the sea!

I went like an arrow from a bow.
My feet flew off that upland ground.
Goat-head and dog-head cursed but found
me impossible to follow.

I have deserved all this:
night-vigils, terror,
flittings across water,

women's cried-out eyes.

One time during his wild career Sweeney left Slieve   68
Lougher and landed in Feegile. He stayed there for
a year among the clear streams and branches of
the wood, eating red holly-berries and dark brown
acorns, and drinking from the River Feegile. At the
end of that time, deep grief and sorrow settled over
him because of his terrible life; so he came out with
this short poem:

> Look at Sweeney now, alas!   69
> His body mortified and numb,
> unconsoled, sleepless
> in the rough blast of the storm.
>
> From Slieve Lougher I came
> to the border marches of Feegile,
> my diet the usual
> ivy-berries and oak-mast.
>
> I spent a whole year on the mountain
> enduring my transformation,
> dabbing, dabbing like a bird
> at the holly-berries' crimson.
>
> My grief is raw and constant.
> Tonight all my strength is gone.
> Who has more cause to lament
> than Mad Sweeney of Glen Bolcain?

One day Sweeney went to Drum Iarann in Connacht   70
where he stole some watercress and drank from a
green-flecked well. A cleric came out of the church,
full of indignation and resentment, calling Sweeney
a well-fed, contented madman, and reproaching him
where he cowered in the yew tree:

Cleric:

> Aren't you the contented one?
> You eat my watercress,
> then you perch in the yew tree
> beside my little house.

Sweeney:

> Contented's not the word!
> I am so terrified,
> so panicky, so haunted
> I dare not bat an eyelid.

> The flight of a small wren
> scares me as much, bell-man,
> as a great expedition
> out to hunt me down.

> Were you in my place, monk,
> and I in yours, think:
> would you enjoy being mad?
> Would you be contented?

72 Once when Sweeney was rambling and raking
through Connacht he ended up in Alternan in
Tireragh. A community of holy people had made
their home there, and it was a lovely valley, with a
turbulent river shooting down the cliff; trees fruited
and blossomed on the cliff-face; there were sheltering
ivies and heavy-topped orchards, there were wild deer
and hares and fat swine; and sleek seals, that used
to sleep on the cliff, having come in from the ocean
beyond. Sweeney coveted the place mightily and sang
its praises aloud in this poem:

73 Sainted cliff at Alternan,
> nut grove, hazel-wood!
> Cold quick sweeps of water
> fall down the cliff-side.

Ivies green and thicken there,
its oak-mast is precious.
Fruited branches nod and bend
from heavy-headed apple trees.

Badgers make their setts there
and swift hares have their form;
and seals' heads swim the ocean,
cobbling the running foam.

And by the waterfall, Colman's son,
Ronan of Drumgesh's victim,
haggard, spent, frost-bitten Sweeney,
is sleeping at the foot of a tree.

At last Sweeney arrived where Moling lived, the place   74
that is known as St Mullins. Just then, Moling was
addressing himself to Kevin's psalter and reading
from it to his students. Sweeney presented himself at
the brink of the well and began to eat watercress.
  – Aren't you the early bird? said the cleric; and
continued, with Sweeney answering, as follows:

Moling: 75
    So, you would steal a march on us,
    up and breakfasting so early!

Sweeney:
    Not so very early, priest.
    Terce has come in Rome already.

Moling:
    And what knowledge has a fool
    about the hour of terce in Rome?

Sweeney:
    The Lord makes me His oracle

from sunrise till sun's going down.

Moling:
Then speak to us of hidden things,
give us tidings of the Lord.

Sweeney:
Not I. But if you are Moling,
you are gifted with the Word.

Moling:
Mad as you are, you are sharp-witted.
How do you know my face and name?

Sweeney:
In my days astray I rested
in this enclosure many a time.

Moling:
But Sweeney, son of Colman Cuar,
why won't you settle in one place?

Sweeney:
The resting place that I prefer
is life in everlasting peace.

Moling:
God help you then. Do you not dread
the slippery brim of hell's wide mouth?

Sweeney:
My one affliction is that God
denies me repose on earth.

Moling:
Come closer then. Come here and share
whatever morsels you would like.

Sweeney:

There are worse things, priest, than hunger.
Imagine living without a cloak.

Moling:

Then you are welcome to my smock,
welcome to my cowl as well.

Sweeney:

Sometimes I recollect
times hurtful to recall.

Moling:

Are you Sweeney, the bogey-man,
escaped out of the fight at Moira?

Sweeney:

I am the early bird, the one
who scavenges, if I am Sweeney.

Moling:

You're mad and sly and know my name
and recognized me. How is that?

Sweeney:

In this enclosure many times
I've watched you from an airy hide-out.

Moling:

Look at this leaf of Kevin's book,
the coilings on this psalter's page.

Sweeney:

The yew leaf coils around my nook
deep in Glen Bolcain's foliage.

Moling:

This churchyard, this whole flush of colour,

is there no pleasure here for you?

Sweeney:
My pleasure is great and other:
the hosting that day at Moira.

Moling:
I will sing Mass and make a hush
of high celebration.

Sweeney:
Leaping from an ivy bush
is a higher calling even.

Moling:
My ministry is only toil,
the weak and strong exhaust me so.

Sweeney:
I toil to a bed up on the chill
steeps of Benevenagh.

Moling:
When your end comes, is it to be
death by water, in holy ground?

Sweeney:
It will be early when I die.
One of your herds will make the wound.

76 – You are more than welcome here, Sweeney, said
Moling, for you are fated to live and die here. You
shall leave the history of your adventures with us and
receive a Christian burial in a churchyard. Therefore,
said Moling, no matter how far you range over
Ireland, day by day, I bind you to return to me every
evening so that I may record your story.

All during the next year the madman kept coming   77
back to Moling. One day he would go to Inishbofin in
west Connacht, another day to lovely Assaroe. Some
days he would view the clean lines of Slemish, some
days he would be shivering on the Mournes. But
wherever he went, every night he would be back for
vespers at St Mullins.

Moling ordered his cook to leave aside some of
each day's milking for Sweeney's supper. This cook's
name was Muirghil and she was married to a swine-
herd of Moling's called Mongan. Anyhow, Sweeney's
supper was like this: she would sink her heel to the
ankle in the nearest cow-dung and fill the hole to the
brim with new milk. Then Sweeney would sneak into
the deserted corner of the milking yard and lap it up.

One night there was a row between Muirghil and   78
another woman, in the course of which the woman
said:

– If you do not prefer your husband, it is a pity you
can't take up with some other man than the looney
you've been meeting all year.

The herd's sister was within earshot and listening
but she said nothing until the next morning. Then
when she saw Muirghil going to leave the milk in the
cow-dung beside the hedge where Sweeney roosted,
she came in to her brother and said:

– Are you a man at all? Your wife's in the hedge
yonder with another man.

Jealousy shook him like a brainstorm. He got up in
a sudden fury, seized a spear from a rack in the house,
and made for the madman. Sweeney was down
swilling the milk out of the cow-dung with his side
exposed towards the herd, who let fly at him with the
spear. It went into Sweeney at the nipple of his left
breast, went through him, and broke his back.

There is another story. Some say the herd had
hidden a deer's horn at the spot where Sweeney

drank from the cow-dung and that Sweeney fell and
killed himself on the point of it.

79   Enna McBracken was ringing the bell for prime at the
door of the churchyard and saw what had happened.
He spoke this poem:

80   This is sad, herd, this was deliberate,
outrageous, sickening and sinful.
Whoever struck here will live to regret
killing the king, the saint, the holy fool.

What good did you expect to come of it?
Repentance will be denied you at your death.
Your soul will go howling to the devil,
your body draw an unabsolved last breath.

But I expect to be with him in heaven,
united in a single strain of prayer.
The soul of the true guest is sped by psalms
on the lips of a fasting, chanting choir.

My heart is breaking with pity for him.
He was a man of fame and high birth.
He was a king, he was a madman.
His grave will be a hallowing of earth.

81   Enna went back and told Moling that Sweeney had
been killed by his swine-herd Mongan. Immediately,
Moling and his community came along to where
Sweeney lay and Sweeney repented and made his
confession to Moling. He received Christ's body and
thanked God for having received it and after that was
anointed by the clerics.

83   *Sweeney:*
There was a time when I preferred
the turtle-dove's soft jubilation

as it flitted round a pool
to the murmur of conversation.

There was a time when I preferred
the blackbird singing on the hill
and the stag loud against the storm
to the clinking tongue of this bell.

There was a time when I preferred
the mountain grouse crying at dawn
to the voice and closeness
of a beautiful woman.

There was a time when I preferred
wolf-packs yelping and howling
to the sheepish voice of a cleric
bleating out plainsong.

You are welcome to pledge healths
and carouse in your drinking dens;
I will dip and steal water
from a well with my open palm.

You are welcome to that cloistered hush
of your students' conversation;
I will study the pure chant
of hounds baying in Glen Bolcain.

You are welcome to your salt meat
and fresh meat in feasting-houses;
I will live content elsewhere
on tufts of green watercress.

The herd's sharp spear wounded me
and passed clean through my body.
Ah Christ, who disposed all things, why
was I not slain at Moira?

Of all the innocent lairs I made
the length and breadth of Ireland
I remember an open bed
above the lough in Mourne.

Of all the innocent lairs I made
the length and breadth of Ireland
I remember bedding down
above the wood in Glen Bolcain.

To you, Christ, I give thanks
for Your Body in communion.
Whatever evil I have done
in this world, I repent.

84   Then Sweeney's death-swoon came over him and Moling, attended by his clerics, rose up and each of them placed a stone on Sweeney's grave.

     – The man who is buried here was cherished indeed, said Moling. How happy we were when we walked and talked along this path. And how I loved to watch him yonder at the well. It is called the Madman's Well because he would often eat its watercress and drink its water, and so it is named after him. And every other place he used to haunt will be cherished, too.

     And then Moling said:

85   I am standing beside Sweeney's grave
remembering him. Wherever he
loved and nested and removed to
will always be dear to me.

Because Sweeney loved Glen Bolcain
I learned to love it, too. He'll miss
all the fresh streams tumbling down,
all the beds of watercress.

He would drink his sup of water from
the well beyond that have called
The Madman's Well; and now his name
keeps brimming in its sandy cold.

I waited long but knew he'd come.
I welcomed, sped him as a guest.
With holy viaticum
I limed him for the Holy Ghost.

Because Mad Sweeney was a pilgrim
to the lip of every well
and every green-banked, cress-topped stream,
their water's his memorial.

Now, if it be the will of God,
rise, Sweeney, take this guiding hand
that has to lay you in the sod
and draw the dark blinds of the ground.

I ask a blessing, by Sweeney's grave.
His memory rises in my breast.
His soul roosts in the tree of love.
His body sinks in its clay nest.

After that, Sweeney rose out of his swoon. Moling   86
took him by the hand and both went towards the door
of the church. When they reached the door Sweeney
leaned his shoulders against the jamb and breathed a
loud sigh. His spirit fled to heaven and his body was
given an honourable burial by Moling.

These have been some of the stories about the   87
adventures of Sweeney, son of Colman Cuar, king of
Dal-Arie.